HERCULES

D0467300

HERCULES

Singing Hands

Delia Ray

WITHDRAWN

CLARION BOOKS
New York

CONTRA COSTA COUNTY LIBRARY

3 1901 04067 1754

Clarion Books
a Houghton Mifflin Company imprint
215 Park Avenue South, New York, NY 10003
Text copyright © 2006 by Delia Ray

The text was set in 12-point Minister Light.

All rights reserved.

For information about permission to reproduce selections from this book,
write to Permissions, Houghton Mifflin Company, 215 Park Avenue South,
New York, NY 10003.

www.houghtonmifflinbooks.com

Printed in the U.S.A.

Library of Congress Cataloging-in-Publication Data

Ray, Delia.
Singing hands / by Delia Ray.
p. cm.
Summary: In the late 1940s, twelve-year-old Gussie, a minister's daughter,
learns the definition of integrity while helping with a celebration at the
Alabama School for the Deaf—her punishment for misdeeds against her
deaf parents and their boarders.
ISBN 0-618-65762-2
[1. Conduct of life—Fiction. 2. Deaf—Fiction. 3. People with disabilities—
Fiction. 4. American Sign Language—Fiction. 5. Family life—Alabama—
Fiction. 6. Clergy—Fiction. 7. Alabama—History—20th century—Fiction.]
I. Title.
PZ7.R2101315Sin 2006
[Fic]—dc22   2005022972

ISBN-13: 978-0-618-65762-9
ISBN-10: 0-618-65762-2

MP 10 9 8 7 6 5 4 3 2 1

For Robert and Estelle
and their daughter Roberta,
who keeps her family's stories alive

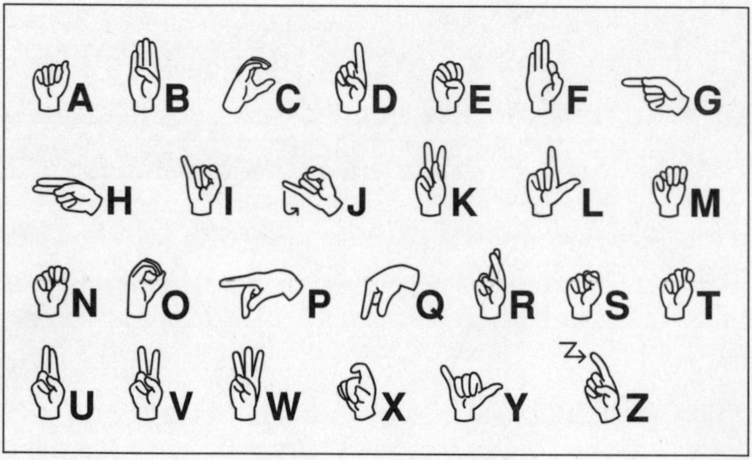
A B C D E F G
H I J K L M
N O P Q R S T
U V W X Y Z

Warmup

Up until the summer of 1948, when I was twelve, probably the worst thing I ever did was hum in church. I started out humming quiet songs like "Beautiful Dreamer," letting the notes ease out in a slow, whispery voice. I would glance sideways and check over my shoulder for any "Ears" who might have slipped into the congregation. Then, if everybody else around me kept staring straight ahead, with their hands folded neatly over their pocketbooks and prayer books, caught up in another one of Daddy's sermons, I would try humming louder. My little sister, Nell, sat beside me with no more than a tiny smile playing along the corners of her perfect red lips. I knew she would never tattle. Nell and I were only fifteen months apart, and we had an unspoken rule: the sister who tattled would endure weeks of shame and loneliness.

After a few Sundays without getting caught, I started humming louder and livelier songs—"I'm Looking Over a Four-Leaf Clover" or "Shoo Fly Pie and Apple Pandowdy." Seeing my lips pressed together tight and a sweet, blank expression locked on my face, no one at Saint Jude's Church for the Deaf had any idea I was holding a private humming concert.

I knew I was probably going too far the day I decided to perform all four verses of "Dixie" right through Holy Communion. But I couldn't seem to stop myself. Nothing else exciting was happening that summer. And it felt heavenly to burst out with noise in Daddy's silent, sweltering church, where the only other sounds were flies buzzing against the windowpanes and the streetcar rumbling along Jefferson Avenue.

I kept humming even when we all started down the aisle toward the altar. Unfortunately, my sixteen-year-old sister, Margaret, had had her fill of my humming. From her usual spot in the back row of the choir, she glared at me as if she could shoot poisoned darts from her eyes. When that didn't work, she threw herself into a small coughing fit to try to get me to hush up. But nobody in the choir noticed her sputtering—not even Mother, who was the unofficial director of the group. She and the other choir ladies were too busy signing the words to the Communion hymn, working to keep their graceful hands in unison.

When Daddy reached my spot at the altar railing, he smiled at me and placed a dry Communion wafer in my cupped palm. I paused "Dixie" only long enough to swallow it, wash down the postage-stamp taste with a sip of wine, and make the sign for Amen. Then, with the most powerful hum I could muster, I started into the refrain—the "Away, away, awaaaaaay down soooooouth in Dixie" part. I winked at Margaret on the way back to my seat. Ha! There was nothing she could do right in the middle of the service—right in the middle of Saint Jude's, smack dab in the middle of a sanctuary packed full of deaf people who worshiped their deaf minister, Reverend Davis, as well as his dear deaf wife, Olivia, and their three lovely hearing daughters, Margaret, Nell, and, in the middle, me—Gussie, secret humming goddess of the South.

Of course, my unusual performance of "Dixie" in church should have been my grand finale that summer, the ultimate test of what I could do without getting caught. But it wasn't. Humming was just the warmup.

1

For a minister's family, church never ends with the last Amen. After services every Sunday, it was our job to stand outside next to Daddy and Mother, nodding and shaking hands with everyone as they filed down the steps. In between smiling and signing good morning, Margaret scolded me. She seemed more annoyed with me than usual, probably because of the heat. Even though it was only June and the beginning of summer vacation, Birmingham already felt like a stew pot. The smell of hot tar drifted up from Jefferson, and I could see tiny beads of sweat gleaming on Margaret's upper lip.

"What were you thinking?" she fumed. "We won't even talk about how sacrilegious you are. But just imagine how horrified Daddy would be if he could hear you. What if somebody's hearing relatives or kids were there? What if the bishop had decided to visit today?"

"All the other kids were in Sunday school," I said. "And there weren't any other Ears around. I checked."

Margaret rolled her eyes with disgust.

Just then I spotted Mr. Runion working his way toward us. He was grinning and bobbing his head, like always. "Oh, boy," I breathed. "Here it comes." Nell let out a little whimper.

For as long as I could remember, old Mr. Runion had tried to make us laugh by shaking our hands so hard and so fast that our arms turned limp as noodles. I know I must have laughed at the trick when I was six or seven. But now, after endless Sundays of being cranked and wiggled and jolted like a jackhammer, I was tired of the joke.

Nell pretended to be coy. She quickly pushed her fist into the pocket of her skirt, but Mr. Runion stood in front of her and held out his hand until she had to surrender. Nell smiled weakly until her turn at arm rattling was over. Mr. Runion let out one of his high, giggly laughs, then moved on to Margaret.

Margaret didn't even wait until he had finished with her before she started nagging me again. "I'm telling you, Gussie," she said, her voice shaking along with her arm, "you went too far today with all that loud humming. I'll have to—"

Mr. Runion was standing in front of me now. But this time I was ready for him. I grabbed hold of his knobby hand and shook back for all I was worth, not letting loose until he pulled away. Mr. Runion looked surprised. He blew on his thick fingers and flexed them as if they had been stuck in a bear trap. "Good grip," he signed, and then moved away.

Nell snickered, but Margaret didn't even congratulate me for setting Mr. Runion straight. She was still lecturing. "I mean it, Gussie," she went on, "if you keep this up, I'll have to tell Daddy."

"Uh-huh, and if you do," I said sweetly, "I'll have to tell Daddy about the time you and Anna Finch sneaked the Communion wine out of the kitchen pantry and had a little tasting party."

"That was three years ago," Margaret snapped, momentarily forgetting to keep smiling and talking through her teeth.

Mother shot us a hard look and Margaret rubbed her hand across her mouth as if she could erase our conversation. Mother's lip-reading skills were legendary. As a young student at Gallaudet, the college for the deaf in Washington, D.C., she had won every lip-reading contest she ever entered.

Mother and Daddy were so good at knowing what we were saying, even when we mumbled or muttered, that I often wondered if they had been playing some sort of strange, elaborate trick on us all these years. Maybe they were just pretending to be deaf, I sometimes thought. Supposedly, Mother had lost her hearing as a baby after a terrible case of scarlet fever, and Daddy told us he had been struck deaf by lightning when he was eight as he stood on his front porch watching a fierce thunderstorm churning up the sky. But just maybe *all those stories were lies.* Maybe they were just waiting to catch us in the act, to catch us when we screamed up and down the stairs at each other before school every morning or played the radio too loud or gossiped about the ladies who rented the spare bedrooms in our big creaky house on Myrtle Street.

Mother gave us another frown, then turned away. "See?" said Margaret. "You're going to get us both in trouble."

I studied Mother's face for a minute, checking to see if anything was amiss. But I could tell she had already forgotten about any problems Margaret and I might be having. As usual, she and Daddy had all the worries of their congregation to attend to. I watched their hands flying and sympathetic expressions flitting over their faces as they patiently greeted one person after another. There was the young Jamison couple, who proudly hovered over their new baby wrapped in two layers of blankets even though it was hot as hell-fire. They wanted to ask Mother endless questions about raising a hearing child. How would the baby learn to talk with deaf parents? When should children be taught to make their first sign?

Then along came Mrs. Thorp, a crabby widow who walked with a jerky limp and had to spend five minutes every Sunday describing the pain in her left heel to anyone who could stand to pay attention. Everyone knew her pain came from stomping on Kanine Kare dog food cans after her snorty little pug, Bertie, finished each meal. But Mrs. Thorp refused to believe that flattening cans could be the cause of her trouble. "I had this limp long before Bertie came along," she claimed, chopping out her words with angry fingers.

I heaved a long sigh. Usually we would be on the way to Texas by now to stay with Mother's sister, Aunt Gloria. Until this year, we had spent most of every summer vacation in Texas. The tradition had started when we were babies, and Mother and Daddy had realized that we might never learn to talk properly if we had only their speaking voices to imitate. So each summer Aunt Glo and Uncle Henry became our substitute speech teachers. Aunt Glo, who could never have children of her own, was more than happy to pour all of her lost years of mothering into two short months with her adoring nieces.

But all that was behind us this year. The As and Bs on our report cards assured Mother that our grasp of the English language seemed to be just fine, and with Daddy gone more and more these days, she hated to give up our company for the whole summer—as well as the extra hands for chores. Then Margaret had to clinch the argument by piping up that she was getting too old to be shipped off for the entire summer, and she couldn't possibly endure the separation from her precious crowd of beaus and girlfriends for that long.

So it was decided. Instead of two months in Texas, we would be staying only one measly week . . . at the end of August. Now the thought of spending the majority of our vacation in humdrum old Birmingham, without Aunt Glo's barbecued spareribs or the lazy afternoons at her country club, made the time stretch out in my mind like an endless desert.

"Who's that?" whispered Nell. A tall, serious man in a striped bow tie had cornered Daddy.

I shrugged. I had never seen him before. Daddy was nodding at him so patiently, even though I knew he must be melting in his stiff white collar and layers of vestments. Then he touched the stranger's elbow and led him back into the sanctuary toward his cramped little office, where he always took people for private conversations.

"Shoot," Nell said, following my gaze. "Guess that means Daddy won't be coming to Britling's with us."

"Nell," I said peevishly, "when was the last time you remember him coming to Britling's Cafeteria with us?" Nell knew that Daddy had only an hour's break before he had to rush across town to hold services for his colored deaf congregation at Saint Simon's.

"I know," Nell said meekly. "I was thinking he might want to since we just got out of school and all, and it's the beginning of vacation and—"

"Huh," I grunted. "Fat chance."

"He can't help it," Margaret cut in. "It's his *job*. He has to take care of people."

"You mean *deaf* people," I muttered. I stared at all the hands flashing around me, moving so fast I could never understand everything they were saying no matter how hard I tried to learn more signs. And the expressions on their faces! They were so . . . so exaggerated, leaping from joy to dismay, barely anything in between. Sometimes I felt as if I had been dropped down in the middle of a secret club, one where my father, Reverend Davis, was president.

I would never belong to the club. I wasn't deaf. I wasn't a natural at signing like Margaret or pretty as a porcelain doll like Nell. And I certainly didn't have the heart full of bounty that Daddy had preached about in his sermon that morning. The only thing I felt like doing was shaking an old man's hand until his teeth rattled.

2

Mother rarely used her voice in public. So my sisters and I froze in surprise at lunch that afternoon when she decided to speak up and ask the waitress for Worcestershire sauce. Her words came out sounding two octaves too high, and garbled, like her mouth was full of marbles. Of course, we Davis girls could understand Mother perfectly. We were used to deciphering her speaking voice, but the waitress looked completely baffled.

She turned to Margaret. "What'd she say?" she asked flatly.

But Mother didn't wait for Margaret to answer. She was angry.

Usually there was no problem at Britling's. In fact, Mother always chose the cafeteria for Sunday lunch because you barely had to ask for a thing. You lined up at the gleaming stainless-steel counter and chose from a selection of roast beef or fried chicken or turkey with all the trimmings. Then you found your seat, and waitresses in spotless starched aprons scurried by with pitchers of iced tea and water.

But our waitress today must have been new. I didn't recognize her, and Margaret and I had already reminded her twice to bring us iced tea, and Nell was missing a fork from her set of silverware. Then, to make matters worse, the condiments—the usual spicy relish, the ketchup, the Tabasco and Worcestershire that Mother loved—weren't on the table.

"Worcestershire sauce," Mother said again, her voice creeping higher and louder. "Worcestershire sauce!" A strange collection of consonants bubbled out of her mouth. The other diners around us were turning to stare.

Mother looked stricken. She was always so dignified, especially on Sunday mornings, outfitted in her best brown silk dress with white polka dots, and her dark hair brushed into neat waves under her hat. But now I could see a flicker of panic in her eyes and a flush spreading over her powdered cheeks.

The waitress put her hands on her hips and said loudly, "Ma'am, I truly have no idea what you're saying. So you can just stop shouting at me whenever you're ready."

Mother closed her mouth, pressing her lips together tightly. She dropped her gaze down to the roast beef and gravy congealing on her plate. It was Nell who hurried to her rescue first. "She said she would like some worsh . . . some woo-chester—" Nell couldn't say it, either. The waitress rolled her eyes.

Right then I hated that waitress more than anyone I had ever hated in my life. I hated her brassy blond hair and the lipstick stuck in the creases of her mouth and the way she kept tapping her pointy pink fingernails on her hips. It wasn't Mother's fault she couldn't speak well. She had lost her hearing long before she ever learned to talk.

I couldn't keep quiet anymore. "She *said*," I yelled across the table, "she wants some steak sauce!"

All at once, the dining room fell completely silent.

"Well, my Lord," the waitress muttered, rolling her eyes again. She spun on her heel, snatched up a bottle of the sauce from a nearby table, and brought it down in front of Mother with a loud thunk. None of us moved until she had sashayed off.

"You shouldn't have yelled at her, Gussie," Margaret said under her breath. Two spots of red still flamed on her cheeks.

"No. Gussie was right," Nell said. "We should complain to the manager."

But Mother shook her head hard, which meant the subject was closed. For a while we sat quietly, trying to eat. Mother didn't touch the Worcestershire. She cut a small, perfect square of meat. Then, after forcing a bite into her mouth, she patted her lips with her napkin and signed that she was going to the ladies' restroom.

Ordinarily I couldn't wait for dessert at Britling's. But now the thought of my usual slab of the chocolate cake with fudge sprinkles or the cherry cobbler topped with whipped cream turned my stomach. I felt as if people were still gawking, and, sure enough, when I glanced at the table where the waitress had fetched the steak sauce, a pair of plump twin girls sat calmly examining us.

I kicked Nell under the table. When she looked up at me, I waggled my fingers and smiled. Nell knew immediately what I was planning.

I signed slowly and elaborately to make sure she would get every word. "There are two girls behind you. . . . Twins. . . . They can't stop staring. Poor things. Not too smart. And they look just like their father. Same red hair. Same frog eyes. . . . But wait. Their brother is very handsome. Maybe sixteen or seventeen. Looks like he has his eye on Margaret."

"Please stop, Gussie," Margaret whispered. "Haven't you embarrassed us enough for one day?"

But of course I wouldn't stop. It wasn't so long ago that Margaret had played the game along with us. Actually, Margaret had been the one to invent the Poor Deaf Girl Game. Together we had spent hours at Morgan's corner drugstore, sitting at the soda fountain, signing dramatically to one another. The object was to see how many people we could fool, how many gullible folks we could trick into pitying us. "Look at those poor deaf-mutes," they would say, or, "See them just a-talking away on their fingers. Wonder what they're going on about."

Then, if we were really feeling devious, we would stop signing and strike up a regular conversation in loud voices, jabbering away over our malted milk shakes, just to let all those people know we had heard every word they said.

But now that she was in high school, Margaret felt as if she had outgrown our old game. "Should I go get Mother?" she threatened quietly.

Nell ignored her. "Does the boy have red hair, too?" she signed back to me.

I swooped my head back and forth. "Oh, no. Black as coal. And eyes as blue as big, fat blueberries." I didn't know the signs for coal and blueberries, so I made a big show of fingerspelling.

Over Nell's shoulder, the girls were still staring, whispering about us behind their cupped hands. I was just getting ready to give Nell another report when I noticed a man at the next table watching me. My heart fluttered in my chest. I recognized him. He was the man from church, the tall one with the striped bow tie. I remembered him talking with Daddy and suddenly realized that, for the last five minutes, I had been signing about the frog-eyed twins and their cute brother, and he must have been reading my signs all along.

"Oh, no," I croaked, reaching for my water glass.

"What is it?" whispered Nell.

"It's the man."

"What man?" Margaret asked, craning her neck over her shoulder.

"Don't look now," I ordered under my breath.

But to my horror, the man was already rising to his feet and coming toward us. He reached our table just as Mother returned from the bathroom. She had powdered her face and composed herself again.

The man touched Mother's shoulder, stopping her before she sat down. "Pardon me," he signed. "I wanted to introduce myself. I was at your husband's service this morning."

Mother smiled and nodded, making a small, pleasant noise in her throat. Then the man began to speak as he signed. His voice didn't sound nasal or muffled—not at all like a deaf person's voice. "I've heard so much about Reverend Davis and followed his work over the years. Today I finally came to see Saint Jude's for myself and ask for your help."

Then he looked directly at me and said, "I've sat through many church services in my time, but never one quite like today's. . . . The musical solo was especially impressive."

3

My humming days were over.

By the time I heard the back screen door bang shut when Daddy came home that afternoon, the truth about what I had done was out. I didn't move. I had spent the last two hours sprawled across my bumpy chenille bedspread, still in my church clothes, waiting for the fan to blow in my direction and for bits of news from downstairs. Nell had been running up with reports every twenty minutes or so.

Now she practically skidded into our bedroom in her sock feet. She closed the door behind her and leaned against it, still huffing from taking the back steps two at a time.

"Daddy's home," she announced ominously.

"I know. I heard the door."

"Mother hasn't told him yet. They're arguing about Daddy's traveling again."

I sat up in bed hopefully. "Really?"

Nell nodded. "Mother says she doesn't care how rich that Mr. Snider from Britling's is or how much money he gives to Saint Jude's. She says Daddy can't possibly add another mission to his list. The church will just have to get somebody else."

"Good." I flopped back on my pillow. Then I popped up again. "But didn't she mention anything about the new car Mr. Snider offered? If Daddy had a car, he wouldn't have to take the train everywhere."

Nell frowned down at me. "I left before they got to that."

I saw her catch a glimpse of her face in the mirror that hung over the dresser between our twin beds. She licked her finger and rubbed at the crease that had appeared between her delicate eyebrows. Then, still gazing at the mirror, she turned her head sideways and fluffed up the light brown curls that swung around her cheeks.

"Stop primping and go see what else they're saying. . . . Please?"

Nell sighed and reluctantly turned from the mirror. "Oh, all right. But you owe me two nights of dish duty for this."

I snorted impatiently. "Fine."

After Nell had gone, I scooted to the edge of the bed and plucked my wrinkled blouse away from my damp back, then refastened my barrettes. Maybe

Mother would be so upset thinking about Daddy's schedule that she'd forget all about my humming.

What wife wouldn't be upset? Daddy was home only one full week a month. The rest of the time he was ministering to deaf people in nine states across the South. Gadsden, Alabama . . . St. Augustine, Florida . . . Meridian, Mississippi . . . Morganton, North Carolina . . . I couldn't even remember all the towns where my father preached. And whenever he was away, it was Mother who had to run things at Saint Jude's.

And now Mr. Moneybags Snider in his striped bow tie wanted Daddy to add *another* town to his list: Macon, Georgia, way off near the middle of the state. Mr. Snider was the son of deaf parents, he had told us right in the middle of Britling's. But even though they were deaf, they had raised him well, he said—so well that he now owned a chain of top-of-the-line furniture stores spread across Georgia and Alabama. He wanted to repay his parents by helping to start a church for the deaf in Macon. "Oh, how my dear mother would love to see that deaf choir signing 'Nearer, My God, to Thee'!" Mr. Snider had exclaimed with tears spilling down his cheeks.

I stepped in front of the mirror and tried to puff my dark hair around my face like Nell's, but it fell in lank clumps to my shoulders. I sighed. I had planned for a transformation in my appearance to occur before I started South Glen Junior High School in the fall. But time was running out. Although I diligently applied Vanish Freckle Fading Creme every night, my freckles hadn't seemed to fade one bit, and my eyebrows were hopeless, stretched out in a fuzzy caterpillar line straight across my brow. Every time I asked Margaret if she would help me tweeze them into pretty arches like hers, she would smirk and say something like, "I'll have to put that on my calendar. Those monsters are gonna take two or three hours, *at least*."

I leaned closer to the mirror, inspecting more carefully. At least I didn't have eyebrows like our upstairs renter Mrs. Fernley. Hers were so sparse she had to fill them in with a brown pencil that left her with two sharp arcs across her brow and a permanent look of surprise. I cocked my head up at the ceiling, listening. She was playing her opera again, just as she had on Sunday afternoons ever since Mother and Daddy had decided to take in roomers last year. I was sure Mrs. Fernley had chosen our house because my parents were deaf and she could play records on her phonograph as loud as she wanted.

Besides being an opera lover, Mrs. Fernley was a divorcee—another fact that made us all a little suspicious, although she was at least fifty and never entertained gentlemen callers. "I enjoy my freedom," I had heard her tell Daddy firmly when she first came to see the room. "The ability to come and go as I please is a luxury that was not possible during my years of marriage."

I couldn't help making fun of the way Mrs. Fernley talked. She spoke as if she might aspire to have a British accent instead of the Southern drawl the rest of us had. At first I thought she spoke in that prim way to help Daddy with lip reading. Then, after several months of listening to her careful enunciation, I decided she was just plain prissy.

She dressed just as carefully as she spoke. Every morning she tip-tapped down our front walkway at eight-twenty to catch the streetcar for downtown Birmingham, where she worked as the chief millinery buyer for Blach's department store. I was fascinated that an adult could have such a job—picking out hats for eight hours each day, week after week. Whenever I could, I rushed to peek out Margaret's window just to see the smart hats or tailored suits Mrs. Fernley wore to work each day.

Then there were the strange odors that wafted down from upstairs whenever she cooked on her hot plate—smoky, musky smells of exotic spices that clung to our clothes and reminded me of the time I stuck my nose in the clove jar when Mother was baking a ham for Christmas.

Mother had a bird-dog sense of smell, and if Mrs. Fernley happened to be cooking, she knew it immediately, even if she was all the way down in our kitchen at the back of the house. She crinkled up her nostrils and pursed her lips with distaste. "Curry!" She spelled out the letters harshly with her fingers, then swept her hands through a scornful combination of signs. "She must have foreign blood."

Just as I was getting ready to apply another layer of freckle-fading cream to the bridge of my nose, Nell burst through the door again.

"Mother told him."

I cringed. "What'd he say?"

"Not much . . . that is, until they called Margaret in and Daddy asked her to tell him the names of all the songs you've ever hummed in church."

"All of them?" I moaned.

"Yep. She even told him about that time you hummed 'Happy Birthday' during the nativity play at Christmas when Mary put Baby Jesus in the manger."

"Gah!" I cried. "That stinking tattletoad Margaret! Did she really have to tell him that, too?"

Nell tried not to smile. I was famous for inventing catchy new insults like "tattletoad." "Daddy wants to see you in his office, Gussie. He sent me up to get you."

I crossed my arms over my chest, plunked myself down on the edge of the bed, and stared stubbornly out at the green shimmer of catalpa leaves just beyond our window.

"You better go on, Gus," Nell said, coming to sit beside me. "Don't worry. How bad can it be? Daddy's so soft, the worst he'll do is probably make you pick dandelions for a couple days."

"Oh, boy," I mumbled, stuffing my feet back into my scuffed oxfords. Once or twice a summer Daddy got it into his head that we needed to decapitate the hundreds of dandelions in our yard, removing the yellow heads by hand before they went to seed and made a hundred more dandelions.

But the thought of what my punishment would be wasn't occupying my mind nearly as much as how I could get back at that goody two-shoes, two-faced, two-timing Margaret.

4

"Good luck," Nell called as I trudged down the hall. I glanced into Margaret's room as I passed. "Jeez," I growled. Just looking at her perfect room infuriated me. I could have gone on and on, listing in my head all the things about Margaret's room that made my blood boil.

1. Penmanship and spelling-bee ribbons tucked into the corners of her mirror. All first or second place.

2. Stuffed lamb, BaBa, always propped neatly against her pillow. Of course he still had his two button eyes and velvety ears even though he was as old as she was.

3. Arrangement of never-overdue library books by her bed. One neat "recently read" stack on

one side. One "still-in-progress" stack on the other.

4. Clear view of the front walkway from large set of double windows with flouncy tieback curtains. Perfect for seeing Mrs. Fernley's latest outfits and spying on the neighbors.

5. Double bed instead of a twin. Plus big, breezy bedroom three feet eight inches wider than the one her sisters had to *share*.

I stopped listing as the sound of Mrs. Fernley's music grew louder. She always turned the volume up for her favorite parts. Now a woman's silvery, mournful voice floated down the dark staircase from the third floor, where Daddy kept his office across the hall from our two renters.

I took my time on the narrow stairs, feeling the temperature rise and hearing the notes climb higher with each step. I had to admit, opera was growing on me a little. I even recognized this one—*Madame Butterfly*. Mrs. Fernley had been thrilled when I asked her the name of it as we passed in the hall one day. She had closed her eyes and sighed, gathering her thoughts, then gone on and on in a trembly voice for nearly ten minutes about "Puccini's masterpiece." I could hear her now behind her door, crooning along with the record.

I paused at the next room down the hall, Grace Homewood's. It was a lucky thing for Miss Grace that she was deaf—in case she didn't care for opera. I pressed my ear against her door to listen. Silence, as usual.

Miss Grace had moved in last year, too, just a week after Mrs. Fernley. Still, I barely knew a thing about her, mainly because she was hardly ever home. She worked at the downtown public library six days a week, shelving and checking out books. And every Sunday her stern-faced hearing parents came over from Mountain Brook, the rich side of town, to take their daughter out to their church and for an afternoon meal. But even when she came home at night, Miss Grace was as quiet as the hushed rows of books at the library where she worked.

I suppose that, besides being deaf, she had good reason to be quiet. Miss Grace was a war widow—a fact that seemed especially unfair considering she was only twenty-four years old and the prettiest woman I had ever seen outside of fashion magazines. Her husband had been shot straight through the heart. It had happened three years ago during World War II, on Okinawa Island near Japan. On the day Miss Grace moved into our house, I caught a glimpse of her husband's photograph when I was helping to carry her boxes upstairs. Corporal Homewood stared out from a silver filigree frame nestled in one corner of a cardboard carton, looking fearless and handsome in his crisp Marine Corps uniform.

Nell and I were constantly begging Mother to tell us every tantalizing detail she might know about the Homewoods. But Mother claimed she knew only two things: Corporal James Homewood had been a hearing man, and he had left for the Pacific just two months after their honeymoon.

At night Nell and I loved to lie in our beds and speculate about Miss Grace's tragic life. Nell fantasized that maybe James wasn't dead but just missing in action somewhere, and any day he might recover from his case of amnesia, find his way home, and come striding up our front walk to retrieve his lovely bride. One night Nell even talked me into turning the lights back on and acting out the couple's reunion. Naturally, I had to play the part of the corporal. When Mother opened the door to find Nell sobbing in my arms, covering me with kisses, she just shook her head and went to bed.

"Augusta?"

I flinched, jerking away from Miss Grace's room. Daddy was standing across the hall in the doorway of his office, watching me. He must have felt the vibration of my footsteps on the stairs. *Augusta.* He always called me by my proper name, which I hated. The only thing I liked about it was that I was named after him—William Augustus Davis III.

"Come sit," Daddy said, motioning me into his office. I could barely hear his voice over the opera music. While Daddy spoke much more clearly than Mother, his deafness always made him sound as if he was straining to get the words out, as if he was constantly recovering from a bad case of laryngitis. "Just a minute," he said, settling himself behind his clunky Smith Corona typewriter. "I just need to . . ." His raspy voice trailed off as he pecked away at the stiff keys, already lost in thought.

If my father wasn't preaching or traveling, he was typing—letters or to-do lists or his next sermon. I plopped down in the cracked leather chair beside his desk to wait. I was glad to sit near the turret of open windows, even though there was barely enough breeze to ruffle the pages of the open Bible or the stacks of papers piled around the desk.

Daddy's office would have been my favorite room in the house except for the fact that it was broiling in the summer and freezing in winter. Like lots of Victorian homes in Birmingham, ours had a round tower that rose along one side of the house and was topped by a pointy, dunce-cap roof. Downstairs, the half-tower in Mother and Daddy's bedroom and in the parlor below were ringed with window seats facing an old crape myrtle tree. Although the tower in Daddy's office wasn't fitted with a seat, you could stand at the wraparound windows, look out over the crape myrtle branches, and see all the way over to Vulcan—Birmingham's most famous statue.

Vulcan was the Roman god of fire and metalworking, and years back some business leaders in town had decided we needed our very own Vulcan to honor all the iron and steel mills in town. If those businessmen had studied Roman myths like we did at South Glen Primary, they might have changed their minds. Vulcan was powerful, but he was also lame and ugly. Now a giant, not-very-handsome statue loomed in cast iron at the top of Red Mountain, keeping watch over Birmingham sprawled below.

Surely, Vulcan would have approved of the temperature in my father's office. I could feel the backs of my knees sticking to the leather seat cushion. Finally, I thumped my foot on the floor to get Daddy's attention. He looked up at me, his gray eyes glazed with concentration.

"Aren't you too hot up here, Daddy?" I asked, swiping my fingers across my brow to make the sign for "hot." The smell of dust and carbon paper and old typewriter ribbons hung over the room like a worn blanket.

Daddy shook his head. He was still in long shirt-sleeves, with his stiff clerical collar fastened tightly around his neck. But like always, he looked cool as marble as he peered at me from behind his spectacles.

"Hmmmmmmmm," he began suddenly. "Hmmm-mmmmmmmmm . . ."

I could feel my eyes grow rounder. Daddy was trying to hum. But of course, it was a tuneless hum. How would he know how to carry a tune if he hadn't heard music—or any other sound—since he was a boy?

Then he stopped just as suddenly as he'd begun. "Is that a godly sound, Augusta?"

I stared back at Daddy blankly.

"Is it?" he asked again. "Is it a beautiful or holy or respectful sound? Is it a sound worthy of Saint Jude's sanctuary?"

"No, sir," I said.

Daddy stared at my lips, waiting for more explanation. When nothing came, he made the sign I had been waiting for. He touched his forehead with his fingers, then brought his fist toward me with his thumb and his pinkie stretched in the shape of a *Y*.

"Why?" he asked out loud.

I couldn't tell Daddy why. He was too good. All around us, fastened on the cracked plaster walls, were dozens of photographs of deaf people he had helped—couples he had introduced and married, men standing in front of the printing press or factory line where Daddy had found them jobs, war veterans who had lost their hearing in battle and who my father had visited in the hospital day after day.

I couldn't tell him I hummed because I was bored silly or because I wanted to see if I could get away with it or because there was this evil little itch way down inside me that I had to scratch once in a while by doing something downright mean.

So I just shrugged. "I don't know why," I whispered.

"Well, I think I do," Daddy said.

"You do?" I asked, glad that he couldn't hear the sharp edge of surprise in my voice.

"Yes," he said. "I do. When Mother told me what you had done, I was angry at first. Then I remembered that one of the most important ways hearing people worship is by singing. . . . I think you just need to sing."

"Sing?"

"I think it's time we sent you girls to the hearing church downtown. The Church of the Advent. You can join the choir there and go to proper Sunday school with a hearing teacher and sing as much as you like. And you can pray out loud and listen to the minister instead of watching the words signed. Mother and I have kept you with us at Saint Jude's too long. You're growing up. You need to worship with other hearing people."

"But, Daddy . . ."

My voice faded away. *He wasn't even going to punish me.* He was so good and so kind that he thought my wicked humming was all about my needing to sing God's praises out loud. It made me want to cry, his sweet smile and the way his clean-shaven cheeks had turned pink with the excitement of this amazing discovery about his daughter.

Finally, I just nodded, swallowing the lump in my throat and feeling more wicked than ever. Daddy rolled his swivel chair closer so he could reach out and pat my knee, then he rolled back to the letter he was composing.

I waved my hand to stop him. "What about Mr. Snider?" I asked too quickly. I made myself slow down. "That Mr. Snider . . . Are you going to do like he asked and try to start another church in Macon?"

Daddy smiled again, but a tired smile this time. A shaft of sunlight glinted off his glasses. "Of course, Augusta," he said. "How can I say no? They need me."

As he went back to typing, I sank into the hot leather chair to watch, wishing for a normal father who could come home for dinner every night or take a nap when he was tired or hear the swell of *Madame Butterfly* drifting down the hall.

5

The very next Sunday, Nell and I found ourselves on the number 51 streetcar bound for downtown Birmingham and the Church of the Advent. At first I resented the idea of being pushed out of Daddy's church, all because of Margaret's big mouth. But now, with the breeze and the smell of mown grass wafting through the streetcar windows and more and more folks climbing aboard at each stop in their starched Sunday best, I felt like I was setting out on a holiday.

Nell didn't seem to share my new burst of enthusiasm. She sat next to me on the streetcar bench, latching and unlatching the clasp of her white basket purse.

"I still don't understand," she whined softly. "If you're the one who did all that humming, why do I have to go to the Advent, too? Why does Margaret get to stay at Saint Jude's?"

"Because Daddy thinks we need to sing," I said. "And didn't you hear?" I mocked in a fawning voice. "Everyone at Saint Jude's would be just beside themselves with grief if they couldn't watch Margaret sign so beeee-eautifully with the choir every Sunday. And what would they do if she wasn't there to fill in when they're short-handed at Sunday school? She has such a *won*derful way with children, you know."

"Why, *yes*," Nell drawled, playing along. "She certainly does."

Frankly, I wouldn't miss working in the Saint Jude's Sunday school one bit. I had only been asked to work there a few times, but that was enough babysitting duty to last a lifetime as far as I was concerned. Instead of coloring Jesus pictures or learning to sign the Lord's Prayer in unison when they were supposed to, most of the kids tore around the church hall like escapees from the zoo. Some were deaf. Some weren't. It didn't matter. One kid made a few signs to another and the next thing we knew, the whole bunch of crazy little rats were making paper airplanes out of the Sunday bulletins.

I looked around happily, inspecting our fellow passengers. "And wouldn't you rather be riding the streetcar downtown than have your arm shaken off by Mr. Runion?" I went on. "Besides, Mother's in charge of another one of those fellowship lunches in the parish house today after the service. Margaret will have to roll all that silverware in napkins and scrub out those nasty deviled squash casserole pans without us." I chuckled slyly.

Nell's mouth spread into a grin. "I guess you're right," she said, smoothing the scratchy hem of my old dotted swiss over her knees. We had both found new hand-me-downs to wear for the occasion. At last I was getting the chance to try out Margaret's frost blue taffeta with the swingy skirt and the mother-of-pearl buttons. Margaret had gasped when I came down for church that morning.

"That's my old spring formal, Gussie! It's way too fancy for church. And besides, it's too big for you. You're swimming in it."

"Well, good," I had called back happily through the screen door as Nell and I set off. "I'll just keep swimming right on over to the Advent. Ta-ta! Have fun at the fellowship lunch!"

I checked my wristwatch. Only five minutes until the nine o'clock service. We could have caught the earlier streetcar if Mother hadn't forced us to eat before we left. Now my breakfast of eggs and toast flip-flopped in my stomach as the car rocked around the circle at Five Points and picked up speed on Twentieth Street, rattling past Daddy's bank, the five-and-dime, and Hillman Hospital. Normally, I wouldn't have minded being late for church, but I didn't want to be too late for our first time at the Advent.

At Morris Avenue, the streetcar stopped to let a Negro family on—three little boys, a mother, and a grandma, all dressed in church clothes. The grandma was huffing, probably from rushing to catch the car. Slowly she heaved herself up the steps, paid the conductor, and made her way panting down the aisle. There were empty spaces up front, where I wished she could sit and rest. But, of course, we had to wait for the whole family to file to the colored section in the very back.

"Put your gloves on," I told Nell as the streetcar started off again. "We're almost there." We weren't used to wearing gloves to church. At Saint Jude's we could never keep them on for very long since they made it too difficult to fingerspell. I snapped open my white patent-leather purse. My gloves were buried at the bottom, under a pile of pennies. Nell leaned over to peer inside my pocketbook as I fished through the jangling change.

"Good grief," she said. "Why'd you bring all those pennies?"

"For the collection plate," I told her. "It's all I had left from my allowance last month. What have you got?"

Nell reached into her plastic change purse and proudly held up two shiny dimes.

"Well, goody for you," I said with a smirk. Nell was a lot better at resisting temptation than I was. I could never leave Morgan's corner drugstore without at least a *True Detective* magazine and maybe a Baby Ruth or a Sugar Daddy. Nell, on the other hand, was oddly happy just to browse through the magazine and candy racks and dream about what she might buy next time.

"Sixth Avenue North!" the conductor called out as he yanked the door lever. It was our stop. I could see the huge carved doors of the Advent across the street. They were already closed. Only a few stragglers were rushing up the wide front steps.

"Hurry," I whispered to Nell. There wasn't enough time to take the crosswalk, so we dashed straight across Twentieth, holding our hats on our heads as we ran.

"Gussie, you're jingling!" Nell panted. "Slow down."

We collected ourselves as we climbed the stairs. Nell bent over to refold her ankle socks. I straightened my hat and repositioned my purse tightly under my arm so the pennies would stop clinking. Then I took a deep breath and hauled open the heavy oak door. Nell scooted in behind me, and for a minute we both stood in the vestibule, letting our eyes adjust to the shadowy light.

"Gee," I heard Nell say softly. The Advent couldn't have been more different from Saint Jude's. Daddy's church was what you would call a no-frills establishment—linoleum floors, whitewashed walls, plain pine benches, and a simple wooden cross hanging behind the altar. Sure, there were a couple of fancy things—the cloth embroidered in gold that covered the altar, and the smooth marble font where babies were baptized. But compared with Daddy's church, the Advent reminded me of an overgrown peacock. Everywhere you looked there was something magnificent, from the mosaic tile floors to the tall stained-glass windows all around us that seemed to glow with ruby red and gold light.

With our shoulders touching, Nell and I moved toward the stone arch that led into the sanctuary. Just as we walked through the opening, a grand-sounding pipe organ and choir exploded into song. Nell craned her neck, searching the vaulted ceilings, as if she thought the music was truly coming down from heaven. But the choir was up front, behind the high pulpit in facing pews, with its members arranged as neatly as chess pieces in their long black robes and white surplices.

I poked Nell in the side with my elbow. "Where should we sit?" I mouthed. The back rows seemed to be filled with babies and toddlers, all being hushed and bounced by their doting parents. At Saint Jude's, parents let their babies whimper and wail till their faces turned blue.

Nell gave a little shrug, scanning the packed pews for space. Suddenly, I felt a hand on my shoulder. It was an old man, trying to tell me something. "Here," he croaked over the music, "let me show you young ladies to a seat. There's an empty place or two up front." We had no choice but to follow his slow, shuffling steps down the wide center aisle. He was so stooped and withered, he looked like he had been ushering folks down church aisles for the last fifty years—without ever taking a break between trips.

I tried to ignore the heads turning as we passed each pew. Nell didn't seem to mind a bit that everyone was staring. She might as well have been Miss Alabama riding on a float in the Cotton Bowl parade, the way she kept smiling at people on both sides. I half expected her to fling up her hand and wave to the crowd.

Finally, I couldn't stand it any longer. I turned my head to see what she was beaming at, and in one glance from right to left, I spotted two kids from her class at South Glen peering over the tops of their hymnals at us. And there was the boy who ran the soda fountain at Morgan's, looking strange in a tie and a fresh crewcut instead of his apron and pointed paper cap. I glanced away before he could catch my eye.

The old man hobbled to a stop at the third row on the right—just as the hymn was ending. He stood patiently waiting for the dark-haired girl at the end of the row to notice us, then slide over to make room. When the girl finally looked up, I felt the corners of my mouth lift in a sickly grin. Missy DuPage. Last year's queen of the South Glen Fall Fun Festival. *What was going on?* Did everyone who went to South Glen have to be Episcopalian? I had thought everybody but us was Baptist or Methodist. And did they all really have to look up at the exact moment that Nell and I were escorted in late, without any family, by the wobbliest usher in Birmingham?

Missy pretended that she didn't recognize me at first. She and her fashion-plate mother and her handsome father and college-boy brother slowly scootched toward the other end of the pew. But I knew Missy was giving Nell and me the once-over as we quickly knelt, then settled ourselves next to them. I could feel her gaze scraping its way along my hand-me-down formal and landing on my skinny shins poking out like Popsicle sticks. Suddenly, the skirt of my dress felt downright poufy, as if someone had blown up the slip with a bicycle pump.

I tried to tuck a couple of handfuls of taffeta under my legs, then opened my prayer book and flipped through the pages, searching for the right place. Nell was looking, too. I waited for Missy or her mother to lean over and whisper the page number, but they didn't move. *Rude,* I thought, my fingers itching to make the sign for "rude" and waggle it under Missy's turned-up nose.

Luckily, Nell found the right page, so I could pay attention to the service and try to forget that I was ten inches away from the festival queen and her perfect family. The minister had begun to read the first Lesson. How easy this was. Most of the time at Saint Jude's, I gave up trying to decipher the meaning of Daddy's prayers and sermons after he swept his hands through the first few signs. His signs were always brightly illuminated by a spotlight carefully positioned above the altar, but the sad truth was that if I focused too long on those lightning hands, I went home with a headache from thinking too hard.

But here I could close my eyes and let the minister's words and the fine voice of the soloist in the choir wash over me. I could understand the message without even trying, and just like Daddy said, I could *sing*. Maybe he was right. Maybe the Advent was the best place for Nell and me after all.

Nell gave me a nudge. "Money."

"What?" I said, blinking back to attention.

"Get your money," she whispered. "They're taking up the collection. Then we're supposed to go out to Sunday school with the other kids."

"Sunday school?" I had forgotten about Sunday school.

"Shhh," she warned. "We go in just a minute. Right before the sermon."

All at once the ancient usher was standing at the

end of our pew again, handing Nell the silver collection plate. It was full of tidy little pledge envelopes
with money tucked inside, but since we were new to
the Advent, we didn't have our envelopes yet. Nell
dropped in her two dimes while I fumbled in the
bottom of my pocketbook for a handful of pennies.
It was hard to pick them up with my gloves on, and I
could feel Missy DuPage peering over my shoulder,
waiting.

I took the collection plate from Nell, trying to slip
the pennies in quick, so that Missy wouldn't notice
my pitiful offering. But she noticed, all right. Working
to get my fistful of coins into the silver plate quietly, I
didn't realize that my purse, still open, was tipping
sideways in my lap. Then I heard it. Everyone heard
it—the sound of pennies striking the hardwood floor
under the pew. Most of them simply scattered, but a
few rolled slowly down the slightly pitched incline
toward the altar. Several folks up ahead turned
around to investigate or looked between their knees
for the source of the sound.

Missy stared at me. She stared as if I was a piece
of dirty bubble gum stuck to the bottom of her shoe.
It was the same look she had given me that day last
year when all the contestants for the Fall Fun Festival queen had gathered on the stage during a school
assembly to hear the principal announce the winner.
There were five of us, and the student body had

voted during the two weeks leading up to the festival by putting coins in glass milk jugs underneath our school pictures. Whoever had the largest amount of money in her jug would not only become queen but would also have the honor of buying the most tickets for needy children to attend the fair free of charge.

Missy had squealed when the principal announced her name. "Our new queen—Missy DuPage!" Mr. Ryker shouted. "Twenty-five dollars and ninety cents!" All the students clapped as he pointed proudly to her jug, which was brimming with nickels and dimes and quarters.

Then, unfortunately, Mr. Ryker had felt the need to list the wonderful contributions earned by the other worthy contestants. "Gussie Davis . . . four dollars and twelve cents." I saw Missy glance in my direction with that bubble-gum-on-the-shoe look. My jug was only half full . . . of nothing but pennies.

And here I was, queen of nothing but pennies again.

I passed the collection plate to Missy, trying to appear unruffled, as if I had just dropped a five-dollar bill on top of the pile of envelopes. But Mrs. DuPage was pointing to a spot in front of Missy's stylish slippers.

"Missy, dear," I heard her whisper, "pick up that penny by your toe for the little girl next to you."

Missy dutifully bent over to fetch the penny, and I

held out my hand to take it. Then, as if I could possibly feel more humiliated, I noticed Missy raise one eyebrow when she looked down at my hand. I looked down, too, and almost gasped. The palm of my glove was filthy, smudged all over with black. I must have run my hand along the banister on my way into church or touched the sides of the streetcar. Why was I surprised? Everything in Birmingham was covered with soot from the steel mills at the edge of town, churning coal dust from their smokestacks around the clock.

Missy dropped the penny into my palm, making sure not to touch any part of my glove. When I murmured "Thank you," she gave a little sniff and turned back toward her mother. No one she associated with would ever show up at church wearing dirty gloves.

With my cheeks still burning, I squeezed the penny in my hand tighter and tighter, as if I could wring blood from copper. The minister was announcing that it was time for all the youngsters to head to their Sunday-school classes. I knew I'd probably be assigned to the incoming junior high class with Missy and all of her snow white–gloved friends.

The truth was I didn't belong at the Advent any more than I belonged at Daddy's church for the deaf. Still, there was nothing to do but stand and file out of the pew behind Nell, stepping over my fallen pennies as I went.

6

I couldn't wait to get to the Cussing Woods after church that day. I hadn't been there since my old best friend, Barbara Blackwell, moved away. Barbara and I used to spend all kinds of time in the vacant lot two blocks from my house. It was there that we discovered how good it felt to say out loud all the bad words we knew—and at the same time whack leaves off the scrubby trees with switches we had made out of sweet-gum branches. We knew only four or five cuss words worth repeating, but even though we had to say the same ones over and over, nothing cured a rotten mood faster than a good round of cussing and switching.

Nell didn't approve of the Cussing Woods. Whenever Barbara and I headed in that direction, she usually stayed behind. But my silence all the way home from the Advent on the streetcar must have worried her. She tagged right along behind me when I stepped off the car and turned toward the vacant lot.

But naturally she couldn't follow me without complaining. "Come on, Gus," she said as we reached the edge of the woods. "Why don't we go home and change our clothes first? Our dresses will get ruined in there."

"Good," I snapped, ducking under a low-hanging branch. "I'm never gonna put this dress on again as long as I live."

Nell stopped a few paces behind me. "Why not? I think it's pretty."

"Then you can have it," I grumbled, yanking a fold of taffeta away from a blackberry bush that hung over our old dirt path. Every summer the little patch of woods seemed to spring to life with honeysuckle, kudzu vine, and pine saplings for a couple of wild green weeks before falling back to its usual scraggly, dusty-looking state.

Nell was still wailing. "But Mother and Margaret will be home soon and wonder where we are. . . ."

"No, they won't," I yelled back over my shoulder. "They've got the fellowship lunch, remember?"

There was no answer. I had come to the little clearing where Barbara and I always stopped to rest and talk when we weren't cussing or switching. Obviously, we weren't the only ones who used the vacant lot. Next to the logs where we used to sit

were old liquor bottles and food wrappers and a
scorched circle of ground where someone had built a
fire. Barbara and I had never worried about the fact
that hobos might be using our woods, too. Somehow
that had only made the lot seem more inviting, more
full of danger and mystery.

Barbara would hold her hand over the pile of ashes
in the little clearing and in a low, ominous voice,
announce, "Still warm. They must have just left."

I dropped my pocketbook on the ground, then
broke off a long sweet-gum branch and began to
strip the leaves, feeling the shame of that morning
come sweeping over me again. The church service
with the spilled pennies and my dirty gloves had
been bad enough. But Sunday school had been even
worse. The teacher, Mrs. Walton, turned out to be a
nosy busybody with darting hawk eyes who immediately asked me, the new girl, to please stand up and
introduce myself to the class.

Since I had chosen a seat at the very back of the
room, the other kids had to turn around in their folding chairs to see me. "Gussie Davis," I said quickly,
pushing myself only halfway out of my seat, then
plopping back down again.

Mrs. Walton forced out a smile. "I'm sorry, dear.
You'll have to stand a little bit longer than that."

I slowly rose, locking my hands in front of my
dress to contain some of its puffiness.

The teacher took a few steps toward me, peering closer. "Gussie . . . That must be a nickname. Can you tell us what it's short for?"

"Augusta," I said softly. I heard someone in the front row trying to smother a laugh.

"And are you new to Birmingham, dear?"

"No, ma'am."

"No? But your family is new to the Advent?"

"Yes, ma'am."

"I don't believe I've had the chance to meet your parents yet. What church did your family attend before coming here?"

I didn't answer right away. Missy and probably plenty of the others had seen Nell and me file into church without any parents. But I knew if I said we had always attended Saint Jude's Church for the Deaf until now, I'd have some complicated explaining to do—something I didn't feel up to at that particular moment, especially when I was wearing that particular dress. So I just stood there.

Mrs. Walton cocked her head, waiting.

My mind scrambled, trying to remember the names of other churches in town. But with everyone gawking at me, it was hopeless. The only thing I could think of was the name of a fancy steakhouse we had passed that morning on the way to church.

"Dear?"

"Delmonico's," I blurted out. "Saint Delmonico's."

Mrs. Walton's eyebrows drew together, making her look more like a hawk than ever. "I see," she finally said after a long pause. She turned on her heel and walked back to the blackboard. "You may sit down now, Miss Davis."

Amazingly, no one in the class had laughed. But I saw the look Missy had traded with the girl sitting next to her. Now, just thinking of it, I couldn't help switching at a nearby clump of brambles and letting loose an evil stream of words—all the ones I had seen scrawled in the bathroom stalls at South Glen, the ones Barbara had taught me, the ones I had overheard when the garbage man had accidentally rammed his truck into a parked car on our street. Over and over I said them.

"Gussie!"

I froze with my switch in midair. Nell was standing on the edge of the clearing with her hands on her hips, the straps of her purse looped over one elbow. Her face was pink and sweaty. "You were practically shouting," she cried.

I let out an exhausted sigh and sat down hard on the nearest log. Nell stepped closer until she was standing over me. "Sunday school couldn't have been that bad," she said. "My class wasn't so awful."

I didn't answer.

Nell put on her cheerful voice. "Maybe next week will be better."

"I'm not going next week."

"Of course you are," she said quickly. "You have to . . . especially after all that cussing." Nell snickered at her own joke. "But, gosh, next time you feel the urge to cuss like that, can't you whisper, or at least do it a little bit quieter? Or—or what about signing? You could *sign* the cuss words instead of saying them!"

"Sign them," I repeated flatly.

Nell nodded, her face shining with the exciting possibilities of her new idea.

"You think there are really signs for those words? And how am I supposed to learn them? Ask Daddy?"

For a brief second, her smile faded; then it reappeared. "You can fingerspell!"

I held my hand over my head and spelled out the D word. "Nope," I said, dropping my fist limply into my lap. "Not nearly as good."

Nell let out a big puff of air. "I give up," she said. She leaned over the spot on the log next to me and tried to brush away the dirt and crumbling bark with the bottom of her purse. Finally, she carefully lowered herself to the edge of the log and perched there, looking around at the scattered trash with disgust.

"This place gives me the creeps, Gussie. There must be people sleeping in these woods at night. And *look*," she said, reaching down to pluck up the folded front page of a newspaper lying near her feet. She dangled it between two fingertips. "This paper is only from a couple of days ago. See! It's the story about that kidnapper who escaped from Atmore Prison Farm."

She glanced anxiously over one shoulder, then the other. "This would be just the kind of place where he would hide," she said, and cringed. "This is probably the paper he was reading to find out how close the police are getting." She dropped the paper as if it had burned her fingers.

I rolled my eyes. "Not Birthmark Baines again," I groaned. Practically everyone in Birmingham was beside themselves with fear that the escaped convict, Horace Baines, who happened to have a large red birthmark splashed across one cheek, would strike again and steal their sleeping children from their beds. Three years earlier Baines had kidnapped the five-year-old son of a bank president in Montgomery and held him for ransom. Fortunately, the police had caught up with him when he was barely a mile down the road with his briefcase full of money.

But two weeks ago Baines had sneaked out of the prison on a delivery truck, and was supposedly armed with a homemade knife and dangerous. He had last been spotted on the outskirts of town, hiding in an old woman's shed. She had called the police, but by the time they arrived, Birthmark Baines was gone.

My parents didn't seem too concerned—a fact that appalled Margaret, especially since Daddy wasn't there to protect us most of the time. Obviously, no right-minded kidnapper would ever target a family like ours if he had hopes of getting a decent ransom. Still, every morning Margaret rushed to fetch the newspaper from the front walk to read the latest reports on Baines, and every night she double-checked the doors and windows to make sure they were locked tight. One evening she even woke Mother up, saying she had heard strange noises. But Mother, who sometimes surprised us with her odd sense of humor, simply said, "I don't hear anything." Then she rolled over and went back to sleep.

"Let me see that," I said, snatching the paper off the ground. I spread out the wrinkled page on my lap and hunched over the article, scanning for details. I read the description in the last paragraph out loud. "Five foot nine, one hundred seventy-five pounds. Last seen wearing a torn green jacket and dark baggy pants. . . ." I let out a high war whoop.

Nell jumped. "What'd you do that for?" she asked.

I sprang to my feet, flapping the newspaper at my side. "I know just what we can do to pay Margaret back for getting us sent to the Advent!" I swiped my switch off the ground and gave the high branch over Nell's head a good whack.

"What *we* can do to pay Margaret back?" she said,

ducking away from the bits of leaves that were raining down.

"You don't even have to help me if you're chick-
en," I crowed. "This is so simple, I can make it work
all by myself."

7

There was only one way to break into Miss Grace's room up on the third floor: we had to steal the extra key from Mother while she was taking her afternoon nap. But Nell didn't seem to understand the logic of my plan or why I might need her help after all.

"I need you to be a lookout." I whispered even though the door to our bedroom was shut tight, just in case Margaret decided to eavesdrop. Her friends weren't due to pick her up for another few minutes.

Nell zipped up the back of her shorts. "Why can't we just use some of Daddy's old clothes to make the Birthmark Baines dummy?"

"Because Margaret has lots of faults, Nell, but being dumb isn't one of them. And Daddy has worn the same kind of black lace-ups and the same black trousers forever. If we used his shoes or pants, Margaret would recognize them in a second."

"Where are we gonna get a torn green jacket like they described in the newspaper?"

"Uhhh!" I grunted with exasperation and lolled my head back against the wall behind my bed. "Don't you see, Nell? We don't need a jacket. That's why this is so simple. Just the shoes and a little bit of the legs are going to be sticking out from under Margaret's bed. It's supposed to look like Birthmark Baines is hiding in her room. Get it?"

"I guess so. But I still don't think it's right to use the clothes of a dead person—especially *a war veteran*—just to play a trick on Margaret."

"I know," I said, gnawing on my bottom lip. "I'm not so thrilled about that part, either. . . . But where else will we get men's clothes? And I know right where Miss Grace keeps the box of her husband's old things. I carried it up myself when she moved in."

"What if she comes home early?" Nell persisted.

"She won't," I snapped. "She's never here on Sundays. She spends the day with her parents, remember?"

Nell didn't answer. She was hunched over the front of her plaid shirt, trying to tie the ends into a knot at her waist like the girl in the Tarzan picture we had seen at the movies last week.

"So will you be my lookout?" I asked again.

"I don't know," she said slowly, plucking at the

long, droopy pieces of shirttail hanging from her knot. She didn't look anything at all like the girl in the Tarzan picture.

"What else have you got to do today, Nell?"

I knew that one would stump her. What to do this summer was a question that had been weighing on our minds a lot lately. In Texas, Aunt Glo had made a point of introducing us to all the wonders of vacation that Daddy was afraid of. "What ever do you mean, your daddy won't let you ride a bicycle?" she cried one day. "Henry, get the Buick! We're going down to the hardware store to buy these girls some bikes!"

Another day it would be "I've signed you up for swimming lessons, sweet girls. You can't spend the summer in Texas and not know how to while away the hours at the country club!"

Aunt Glo still wrote us each a letter every week. "As much as I hate to say this," she had written in my last one, "your mother—my *baby* sister, Olivia— is not only hard of hearing. SHE IS HARD OF HEAD!!!!!! One pitiful week in the dead of August with my precious girls can hardly be called a proper vacation. *But she will not relent!!*"

I couldn't help dripping tears on the letter. At least Margaret had friends who could drive and take her places. Nell and I were stuck wandering around our stifling old house, waiting for instructions from

Mother or inspiration for how to fill the long hours between chores. That was why making the Birthmark Baines dummy was such a clever idea. How else would we occupy our time all afternoon?

I looked up at the faint sound of a car horn beeping. "Come on," I said, pulling off my shoes and bouncing up from the bed. "That's Margaret's ride. And Mother's sure to be asleep by now. Let's get started." I opened the door and stuck my head out, listening.

"Bye!" Margaret shouted up the stairs. "Tell Mother I'll be back in time for supper!"

"All right! See you then!" I called down, and waited for her to pull the front door shut. I tiptoed into the hall, glad when I felt Nell come padding up behind me. We crossed in front of the stairway and stopped outside Mother and Daddy's bedroom door. Luckily, Mother had left it open a crack. I could hear the sound of her snoring—soft and rhythmic—beyond the door.

I reached out one finger and pushed the door until it swayed open with a loud creak. Nell crouched lower, wincing. "Careful," she whispered.

I glared at her over my shoulder. Who was she telling to be careful? No one knew better than I did how hard it was to sneak past Mother—even when she was snoring. Supposedly, when we were newborn babies, Mother had always insisted that we sleep with her at night, pinned to her side with a cloth diaper that would tug her awake in case we cried or flailed about. But I never understood why Mother thought she needed the diaper. Most of the time, she dozed like a cat, with her eyes ready to flicker open at the slightest vibration.

So I had no choice. In order to make the journey across the bedroom to the dressing table where Mother kept the key, I would have to slither on my stomach, snake style. I checked Mother one more time. She was still breathing deeply, with her *Ladies' Home Journal* laid open across her chest.

Poor thing. She hadn't even taken the time to change out of her church dress or her hot stockings. Like most Sundays when Daddy was traveling, she had come home from Saint Jude's exhausted after a week of getting out the church bulletin, organizing the choir and the service, and planning the fellowship lunch. And as if *that* wasn't enough, she told us before she swallowed her headache medicine and went off to bed, that persnickety Mrs. Thorp had had the gall to complain that the baked ham was too dry.

I dropped onto all fours, then slowly lowered myself to the hardwood floor. The dressing table was over near the window seat, only a stone's throw away, but before me lay a minefield of obstacles—a stack of old *Ladies' Home Journal*s, two hooked throw rugs, a laundry basket full of folded clothes, and Mother's high heels. I started at a creep, stopping every couple of feet to peer in Mother's direction, or when I heard Nell suck in her breath as my foot moved dangerously close to the leaning stack of magazines. But once I had passed the bed and the hooked rugs, I picked up speed, sliding the worn knees of my dungarees along the smooth floorboards.

When I reached the dressing table, I carefully pushed myself up on the pink satin stool and gave a little wave to Nell's cloudy reflection in the old mirror. She swiped her hand at me, telling me to hurry up. But I couldn't rush this last part. Bit by bit I inched the narrow drawer of the vanity open. I let out a sigh of relief when I saw the keys on the ring labeled "3rd floor" resting in their usual place next to Mother's cameo brooch and pairs of clip-on earrings. Graceful as a ballerina, I fished up the key ring with one finger and smoothly slid the drawer shut again. Then, for a final flourish, I turned and jingled the keys at Nell.

"Stop it!" she mouthed, squeezing her small hands into fists and hitting the air.

"Why?" I asked out loud.

Nell froze. Her eyes filled with panic.

"She can't hear us, remember?" I said. I stood perfectly still, calmly dangling the key ring from my finger. "See? She's snoozing away. We just can't make—any—vibrations—" Nell looked as if she might wet her pants. I clapped my free hand over my mouth to hold back a burst of laughter.

"I'm leaving!" she said in a strangled whisper. But just as she started to turn, the doorbell rang.

On its own, the doorbell wouldn't have been much of a problem. But in our house, whenever the bell rang, specially wired light bulbs scattered throughout the first and second floors flashed on and off to let our parents know when someone had come to call. In Mother's room the light bulb happened to be fixed to the wall directly over her bedside table.

Now it was my turn to freeze. I stared at Mother, waiting for her eyes to pop open when the light bulb blinked.

"Get the door!" I whispered frantically to Nell, and dropped to my knees as she turned and tiptoed toward the staircase. With the keys clenched in one hand I shimmied toward the hallway, praying for Mother to stay asleep. I could hear Nell downstairs greeting someone, her voice sounding strangely high and full of cheer.

Just as I reached the side of her bed, Mother stirred. I felt her above me rolling over on her side, and the next thing I knew, her magazine had slid onto my head. I let out a little yelp. And now Nell was coming up the steps with whoever had rung the bell. Mother's door was wide open, and there I was sprawled on the floor in clear view. What else could I do?

I wriggled under the bed.

"What a featherhead," a woman's breathless voice was saying. "I went to work this afternoon to catch up on some accounts, and I must have left my keys sitting right on my desk at the office." It was Mrs. Fernley. It sounded as if she and Nell had stopped on the landing.

"But I'm perplexed," she went on. "In the entire time I've been living here, I never remember your parents keeping the front door locked."

"Oh, that must have been Margaret who locked up," Nell told her. "She's terrified about that escaped convict sneaking in here to kidnap us. You know, the one from Atmore? Birthmark Baines?"

I could feel a drop of sweat trickling down my hairline. Slowly I laid my cheek on the gritty floor and blew at a dust ball that had settled near my nose. Thank goodness the box springs above me had stopped creaking. Mother must have dozed off again. But Nell was *still* stalling on the stairs, probably trying to keep Mrs. Fernley on the landing while I ran for cover.

She rattled on and on. "That's right. Margaret's an awful worrywart, but I guess you can't blame her. People say he could be hiding anywhere in Birmingham. Maybe right in this neighborhood . . ."

"Oh, I'm sure Margaret needn't worry about this Baines character," Mrs. Fernley said rather impatiently. "This is a very safe neighborhood. I really only lock the door to my room out of habit. . . . Now, dear, I do hate to disturb your mother, but if you'll please just go and ask her for the duplicate of my key."

"Are you sure you don't want to wait downstairs where it's more comfortable?" Nell asked nervously. "This might take a while. Mother's awfully hard to wake up from her nap sometimes."

"I see," Mrs. Fernley said. "Well, I think I'll just wait for you upstairs. Please apologize to your mother for the interruption."

"Yes. I'll be sure and do that," Nell announced loudly. Then I heard her rush up the stairs ahead of Mrs. Fernley. I could see her legs from my spot under the bed. She had planted herself in front of Mother's doorway.

Once Mrs. Fernley was on her way to the third floor, Nell tiptoed into the bedroom. "Gussie?" she hissed.

I thrust my hand with the keys out from under the bed and jingled them. Nell snatched them away, then scrambled toward the dressing table. Over my head the box springs gave a sudden squeak. I held my breath, waiting for the worst, but Nell must have heard the noise and wheeled around in time to see Mother sitting up in bed.

"Oh, you're awake!" Nell practically shouted. She took a few steps closer so Mother could read her lips. "I was just getting the keys from your drawer for Mrs. Fernley. She's locked herself out of her room."

Mother's stocking feet appeared beside me, resting lightly on the floor. Her voice sounded woozy with sleep, even fuzzier than usual. "Locked out? Why didn't you come get me?"

I knew Nell must be signing as she explained. I could hear the keys jingling. "You were so tired. I didn't want to bother you."

"It's all right," Mother said, getting to her feet. I clenched my arms closer to my body, trying to make myself smaller. "You go take the keys to Mrs. Fernley. I just need to splash some water on my face."

Nell hurried off as Mother shuffled toward the bathroom down the hall. I waited to hear the door close behind her and the rush of water filling the sink. It was simple, almost *too* simple, to crawl out from under the bed, dust myself off, and slip from her room unnoticed. Maybe if it had been more difficult in the end, I would have dropped my farfetched plan for getting revenge on Margaret. But we had the keys now. We even had Mother's permission to take them!

Yes, there was no doubt about it. The Birthmark Baines dummy was meant to be.

8

I didn't have second thoughts about my plan until I saw Corporal Homewood staring up at me from the box in Miss Grace's closet. His dark eyes gazed out from the same silver-framed photograph I had caught a glimpse of the first day Miss Grace moved in. I had expected that the picture would be on display, on the dresser or the bedside table. But now, here it was, still nestled in the cardboard carton on top of his old things. No wonder she's hidden the picture away, I thought. It would make her too sad to look at her dead husband's face every day.

Even though it was warm and stuffy in Miss Grace's little room on the third floor, a cold chill prickled along the back of my neck. Still kneeling by the closet, I glanced over my shoulder into the dim corners. I hardly knew Miss Grace, but I could feel her all around me. A faint trace of the rose water she wore hung in the air. And strands of her white-blond hair trailed from the enamel brush sitting on the small table next to her neatly made bed. How perfect they must have looked together, the corporal with his dark hair and eyes, and Miss Grace so small and fair.

I felt a little better once I started trying to make sense of the objects in the room. Kneeling there, I felt like I was finding the lost parts of a jigsaw puzzle. I hadn't known that Miss Grace went to the Alabama School for the Deaf like Daddy did when he was young, but there was her ASD diploma hanging on the wall over her desk. My father paid visits to ASD often to hold chapel services for the students there. He had probably met Miss Grace on one of those trips.

Nell would be sorry she had turned chicken and refused to be my lookout. She was probably flopped on the glider on the front porch now, bored senseless and sulking over how I had snatched the third-floor keys from her hand and called her a yellow-tailed crybaby. I didn't need Nell to stand watch anyway. It was only two o'clock. Miss Grace's parents wouldn't bring her home from Sunday dinner for at least another couple of hours.

I stood up and tiptoed over to the tidy desk for a closer look. It was almost bare except for a pile of blank stationery stacked in the middle with a small wooden paperweight perched on top. I carefully picked up the paperweight and set it down again, admiring the unusual design and the smooth ridges in the wood. It was shaped like a perfect, small hand, pressing whatever was underneath into order.

The only other object on the desk was a framed photograph of a young couple gazing down at a tow-headed toddler in her father's arms. The baby girl was wearing a sunsuit and beaming at the camera. Her mother was on the verge of laughing, tickled with some clever thing her child had just done. I bent closer. Was that a picture of Miss Grace with her parents when she was little? I hardly recognized those delighted faces. Miss Grace's parents seemed as cold as stone whenever they came to fetch their daughter on Sunday mornings. Several times I had peeked around the drapes in the parlor to see them sitting at the curb in their long black Oldsmobile, staring blankly ahead until Miss Grace slipped out of the house to meet them.

Once, Mother had joined me at the window to watch over my shoulder as they drove away. "Why don't they ever come up on the porch to say hello?" I had asked.

"They're hearing," Mother had signed. Then she had added another little gesture—a quick brush of her finger under the tip of her nose while she pursed her lips, as if she had just bitten down on something sour. I knew what she meant. Miss Grace's parents were Uppish Hearing. Too high and mighty to try to communicate with simple deaf folks like Mother and Daddy, who lived on the wrong side of town and rented out rooms on the third floor.

"But what about Miss Grace?" I had asked, pushing for as many answers as I could get before Mother grew impatient. "Their own *daughter* is deaf."

Mother had shrugged as she signed. "They can't stop wishing she wasn't."

I had frowned, lifting my hand to fire out more questions. But Mother had already turned away from the window and was rushing off to clear the breakfast dishes from the table.

I moved back to the box of Corporal Homewood's things, feeling a little squeamish as I suddenly remembered my mission: to get a pair of trousers and shoes for the Birthmark Baines dummy. Mrs. Fernley's opera music seeping through the back wall of the closet didn't help to calm my nerves. It was a recording I had never heard before—something wild and frantic, with dueling voices and clashing cymbals that made me think of armies charging into battle. My heart thumped along with the music as I set the corporal's photo aside and fumbled through the box, searching for what I wanted. On the top of the pile were a striped necktie and a fine gray wool suit, with suspenders still buttoned to the pants and traces of a sharp crease running down the front of each leg. Too swanky for Birthmark, I decided, and carefully laid the suit on the floor. Next came a worn baseball mitt and a white sweater with a blue border around the V-neck—the kind I had seen tennis players wearing at Aunt Glo's country club. No help.

A red silk bathrobe. No.

Flannel pajamas. No.

Growing impatient, I yanked out the next piece of clothing in the pile and then caught myself as I slowly realized what I was holding. It was the military jacket Corporal Homewood was wearing in his photograph. My hands tingled as I laid the dark blue jacket in my lap and ran one finger over the gold buttons and the colored military badges still fastened over the breast pocket. An awful thought crept into my mind, and I leaned closer, examining the pocket for holes. He had been shot through the heart. What if this was the jacket he had been wearing?

"Snap out of it, Gussie," I whispered. This was his dress uniform. He would have been wearing soldiers' fatigues on Okinawa. I closed my eyes for a second, then thrust my hand down to the bottom of the box and pulled out the matching pants of the uniform.

I groaned under my breath. They were light blue with red trim. I'd never be able to pull off Birthmark Baines with a pair of marine pants. Feeling defeated, I returned the clothes and the photograph to the box, making sure to get them in the right order.

Then I shut the cardboard flaps and shoved the carton back into the closet. I was giving the closet one last look to make sure nothing was out of place when I noticed the stack of shoe boxes on the top shelf.

Shoes! I had almost forgotten. If I just had some halfway convincing men's shoes to stick out from under Margaret's bed, maybe I could make my trick work after all. I stood on the tips of my toes and pulled down the boxes. Mrs. Fernley's music was getting louder, practically vibrating Miss Grace's clothes hangers on the rod as I lifted the lids on sandals and high-heeled pumps and rain galoshes.

I was tempted to give up after the disappointing set of screwdrivers under the fourth lid, but there was one shoe box left at the far end of the shelf. And now through the wall I could hear a huge cast of singers joining in with the orchestra, their triumphant voices soaring and urging me on to victory. I dove back into the rising cloud of mothball dust and lavender sachet and reached for the last box. My heart sank at first. It felt much too light to hold the heavy leather clodhoppers I was looking for. Just to make sure though, I opened the lid.

Of course I knew it was wrong. Of course I shouldn't have been in the room in the first place. I shouldn't have been digging through a dead soldier's last earthly possessions. And I definitely shouldn't have perched myself on the edge of Miss Grace's bed and pulled the end of the ribbon tying the stack of old letters in the shoe box together. But there were no envelopes hiding the letters, and she was such a mystery to me, and here were all the clues to her lost life with Corporal Homewood at my fingertips.

With trembling fingers, I flipped through the stack. "My Dearest Grace," the letters began. They were written on faded light blue paper and dated 1944 and 1945, the exact years when her husband would have been half a world away at the front, fighting the Japanese and writing his wife from some lonely tent or foxhole. I stopped at the last letter, which was no more than a paragraph long, and read greedily:

February 12, 1945

My Dearest Grace,

In your last letter you said that each word I write only makes our separation more painful. But how can I stop writing? Our letters are the last tie binding us together—the only good to come out of this long, vicious war.

My sincerest hope is that you will write again.

Vincent

I gasped. *Vincent?* Who was Vincent? Corporal Homewood's name was James! I scanned the letter again, not wanting to believe it. But there it was, plain as day, "makes our separation more painful." I turned back to the first letter in the stack and checked the signature. Vincent. The next letter was signed Vincent, too. But how could Miss Grace have loved someone else?

I wanted to read more, to search for an explanation, but I knew I had stayed too long already. So I didn't have a pair of men's shoes when I quietly slipped from Miss Grace's room and locked the door behind me. Or even a pair of suitable Birthmark Baines pants. But I had one very shocking and mysterious letter from the bottom of the secret bundle to discuss with Nell . . . if I ever decided to speak to her again.

9

Forgiving Nell for turning chicken was the easy part. Showing her the letter proved to be more difficult. I was dying to share what I had found. But somehow once I was downstairs again, away from Mrs. Fernley's pounding battle victory music and in the cozy quiet of our bedroom, I knew I couldn't tell anyone what I had done. All of a sudden even *I* was shocked at the thought of Miss Grace's letter tucked down inside the pocket of my dungarees. What had I been thinking? Nell would be appalled. Genuinely scandalized.

"So you didn't find *anything* for the dummy?" Nell asked as I sat on my bed inspecting a broken fingernail.

I shook my head.

"No pants, no nothing?"

"Nope," I said.

Nell crossed her arms over her chest, studying me suspiciously. "You sure were up there a long time."

"Well, I didn't find anything," I shot back. "All right?"

I swiped a Nancy Drew mystery off the dresser, then threw myself back on my bed and pretended to read *The Hidden Staircase*. After a while, Nell wandered away. As soon as she was gone, I lurched to my feet and fished the letter out of my pocket, searching the room for somewhere to hide it. My old sewing basket sat forgotten in the corner. Quickly I stuffed the letter underneath a tangled needlepoint sampler I had never finished. Once I figured out a way to sneak back up to Miss Grace's room without anyone noticing, I'd return the letter and try to forget any of this had ever happened.

I was just closing the lid of the basket when Nell flew back into the room, her eyes shining with excitement and her arms wrapped around a lumpy bundle of clothes.

"What's that?" I asked.

"Everything you need for Birthmark Baines," she said happily. "You looked so pitiful when you came down from Miss Grace's room. I decided I should help you after all." She dropped the bundle on my bed, and a pair of shoes I had never seen before rolled out.

They were snazzy brown and white buckskins that

looked like something an old-timey college boy out on the town would wear. "Where'd you get those?" I asked.

"Daddy's closet," Nell declared triumphantly. "And look." She held up a pair of baggy khaki trousers. They were covered in paint stains, with a rip on one knee. I vaguely recalled seeing Daddy wear them when he organized a team of men to paint the parish house.

"Can you believe he ever wore these?" Nell asked. "Aren't they perfect?"

I started to laugh. "The pants are okay, Nell, but those shoes will never work."

Nell gave a little stomp with her foot. "You said we needed something that did *not* look like Daddy," she huffed.

"Well, gah, Nell, do you think Birthmark Baines would go around kidnapping kids in buckskin dancing shoes?"

Her face flooded with disappointment. I hadn't meant to sound so ungrateful. I reached for the shoes and held them up at arm's length. "But you never know," I said slowly. "Maybe . . . maybe these do look like what a convict would wear to disguise himself."

Nell brightened a little. "Really? So you think we should go ahead with the plan?"

"Sure," I said. "Why not?"

No sooner had the words left my mouth than we heard Margaret coming through the front door.

"Dadgummit!" I said. "What's she doing home already?"

Nell heaved a huge sigh. "Oh, never mind. Let's just forget about the dummy. It wouldn't have worked anyway."

"Nope," I said stubbornly. "We're gonna do it. But we don't have time to stuff a dummy now. I'll have to be Birthmark Baines."

"You *what?*" Nell's eyes widened as she watched me yank Daddy's trousers off the bed and hold them up to my waist.

"You'll see. But first go listen at the top of the steps and make sure she's not coming up here."

Once I had shooed Nell into the hall, I quickly pulled the paint-stained pants over my dungarees. But even with my own clothes underneath, the pants looked too long and floppy. Daddy was taller than I thought. Hitching up the waistband in one fist, I waddled over to our dresser and yanked the top drawer open to reveal piles of silky slips and training bras and no-nonsense cotton underwear. I never knew Aunt Glo's undergarment obsession would come in so handy. "You can never have enough clean underclothes, girls," Aunt Glo would remind us at the beginning of every stay in Texas before she carted us off to Conway's department store for another shopping spree in the girls' department.

Now I grabbed handfuls of underwear and stuffed them down the pants until the trouser legs began to fill out and appear slightly more manly.

Nell was standing in the doorway again. "What in the world are you doing now?" she asked breathlessly, staring at the pairs of panties clenched in my fists.

"I need more padding!" I cried. "Come help me."

Nell scurried over to shove more underwear up around my shins. She fluttered about my bottom half like a lady in waiting as I started shuffling toward the door.

"What about socks?" she asked.

I grabbed Daddy's shoes off my bed. "If Baines can wear bucks," I said, "I suppose he can wear white bobby socks, too."

"Now, listen," I went on. "I'm gonna get under Margaret's bed. All you have to do is go downstairs and tell Margaret you found the back door wide open while she was gone and you just heard strange noises coming from her bedroom. If she asks where I am, tell her I've been at the vacant lot all afternoon. Mother should be cooking dinner, so she'll be too busy to see what you're saying. Okay? Have you got it?"

Nell was eyeing my lumpy trouser legs doubtfully. "This isn't going to work, is it?"

I shrugged. "Probably not, but it's worth a try. Margaret's been looking for escaped convicts around every corner. Now she's finally gonna get one." I grinned and waddled down the hall toward Margaret's bedroom with a buckskin tucked under each arm.

Nell watched me from the top of the stairs. "Just give me a couple minutes to get myself situated," I whispered over my shoulder.

Getting situated was not as easy as I thought it would be. By the time I had propped my feet in Daddy's shoes, squeezed myself partway under Margaret's bed, rearranged my underwear padding, and strategically placed my legs so that they looked halfway convincing, I was worn out. Margaret's bed wasn't nearly as high as Mother and Daddy's. The musty-smelling box springs were barely two inches from my nose. To make matters worse, a hook on a training bra was poking like a needle into my rear end—but every time I tried to wiggle around to adjust it, Daddy's heavy bucks would flop off my feet and bang on the floor.

At last I managed to fish the shoes back on with my toes and lie still for a few minutes. I couldn't help being impatient. This was the second time in one day I had found myself under a bed, struggling to stay as stiff as a corpse, when what I really needed to be doing was sneaking back upstairs to return Miss Grace's letter before she came home.

"Come on, Margaret," I muttered. I had broken into a sweat inside the two pairs of pants and all those layers of underwear. I wasn't sure how much longer I could stand it. I felt like I was in a coffin . . . skewered and roasting on brassiere hooks in a very narrow, dusty coffin.

I took a deep breath to calm myself. What could Nell possibly—

All of a sudden, an earsplitting shriek rang out above me. My heart leaped into my throat, and I could feel a thrill of victory shooting through my veins like delicious, thirst-quenching ice water. I couldn't believe it had worked.

"Hel-l-lp!" the shrieking went on. "Good Lord in heaven above! Girls, come *quick!*"

I froze. That wasn't Margaret screaming. It was Mrs. Fernley. How could I have forgotten? Mrs. Fernley always washed her hair in our second-floor bathroom on Sundays, then set it in pin curls to get herself ready for the week ahead. She must have heard my bumps and thuds and come across the hall to investigate. And she was nearsighted, so if she had left her eyeglasses upstairs in her room . . .

"Wait!" I called weakly. "Mrs. Fernley, it's me. Just wait." I was wedged in too tight to roll over and crawl from under the bed. I had to push my way out feet first, inch by inch. But even when I felt Daddy's shoes thud to the floor again, Mrs. Fernley kept screaming. Now I could hear her running to the top of the stairs.

"*Girls!*" she shrieked again. "Mrs. Davis! *Anyone!*"

Finally, I was out. I clambered to my sock feet and lurched toward the hallway, yelling as I ran. "It's me!" I shouted, bursting out of Margaret's room. "It's Gussie!"

Mrs. Fernley, in a cold-cream mask and a damp silk kimono, wasn't the only one who turned to stare at me with a horrified gaze. Nell was on the stairs, too, and right behind her, Margaret, and right behind Margaret, Preston Tucker, six-foot-two varsity basketball star of South Glen High and the date of my older sister's dreams.

For a minute, Preston Tucker's wide mouth hung open like everyone else's. But then I saw his gaze land upon my sagging, paint-stained pants and the silky trail of slips, bras, and underpants strewn behind me, and he started to smile.

What was there to say? I closed my mouth, hitched up my pants, and hobbled to my bedroom, shutting the door quietly behind me.

10

Knavery
Imprudence
Impropriety
Mortification
Perfidy
Ignominy
Acrimony

It was not until after dinner the next evening that Mrs. Fernley summoned me to her room and grandly placed the neatly typed list of words in my hands with a smile as if she was presenting me with a box of chocolates. I squinted down at the crisp onion-skin paper, trying to make sense of all those syllables. I recognized only one word—"mortification"—which, obviously, Mrs. Fernley and I (and Margaret, too, I suppose) had experienced in front of Preston Tucker the evening before. But it wasn't very difficult to see that the other rather evil and unpleasant-looking words were mainly meant to describe me and the nature of the trick I had tried to play.

Mrs. Fernley waited for me to look up and meet her pointed gaze. "You know, Gussie," she said, arching one of her penciled-on eyebrows, "before becoming head millinery buyer at Blach's, I used to be a high school English teacher"—she paused dramatically—"for twenty-one years."

I felt my mouth drop open in surprise. Mrs. Fernley didn't look or act like any teacher I had ever known. I couldn't imagine a single one of the faculty members at South Glen wearing a feathered hat and crimson lipstick to work or owning a kimono with a Chinese dragon embroidered on the back or listening to opera every spare minute.

And they certainly would never decorate a room the way Mrs. Fernley had. I remembered how irked Mother was when Mrs. Fernley asked if she could move our plain maple bedroom set down to the cellar to make space for her own showy furnishings. I sneaked a sideways glance at her tasseled burgundy lampshades and the tall wooden screen hiding her hot plate in the corner. It was painted with splashy lilies and some sort of long-necked bird holding a fish in its mouth.

But there she was, sounding more and more like a teacher with every word that came out of her brightly painted lips. "I've seen all manner of adolescent antics in my day, Gussie," she continued. "So when I went downstairs to confer with your poor hearing-impaired mother about your punishment last night, I did my best to assure her that I would take care of this the same way I used to take care of such shenanigans back in my teaching days. With a weekly word list."

"Word list?" I repeated faintly.

"That's right." She gave a curt nod. "I'm aware that your mother has also assigned you extra duties around the house. . . ."

I lifted my chin and gave a tragic little sniff, thinking of all the silver and furniture polishing I was in for over the next two weeks. Of course, I took all the blame and didn't tattle on Nell for her part in our scheme when she swiped Daddy's clothes for my disguise. In return, she had offered to help with my chores. I was pleased with myself for refusing her help and making her feel even worse.

According to Margaret, Nell must have completely forgotten about me yesterday once she spotted Preston Tucker sitting on the davenport, drinking iced tea. Instead of following through with our plan, my little sister had commenced flirting with Preston. It wasn't until Mrs. Fernley started screaming that she even remembered me broiling under the bed upstairs.

But the crowning blow had come that morning

when I was downstairs dusting, and Mother must have asked Nell what she had done with the extra set of keys to the third floor. Nell had run directly to our bedroom to fish them out of the pocket of my dungarees and hand them over to Mother, completely ruining my chances of returning Miss Grace's letter any time soon.

Mrs. Fernley was still lecturing on the benefits of her word list. "I do think my method might get at the heart of the problem much more directly than mindless chores," she was saying. "I expect you to define the words on this list and then use each one in a well-crafted sentence as you reflect on your behavior. My hope, and I'm sure the hope of your parents, is that in contemplating these words, you might begin to act more thoughtfully and weigh the results of your actions before making such misguided decisions. Do you understand?"

I looked down at the paper in my hands, hesitating before I answered.

"The first word, for example," Mrs. Fernley said. "'Knavery.' Do you know what that means?"

I shook my head.

Mrs. Fernley spun around and tip-tapped across the crowded room to a bookshelf wedged next to her bed. She bent down to one of the lower shelves and with a theatrical grunt hefted up the largest book I had ever laid eyes on.

"You'll need to sit down," Mrs. Fernley huffed,

nodding toward a love seat covered in plush pink velveteen. Once I had set the word list on the gold-leaf coffee table and leaned back against the cushions, she carefully lowered the worn book with its frayed cloth binding into my lap.

"Wow," I wheezed. The book must have weighed more than ten normal-sized books put together.

"The *Funk and Wagnalls New Standard Dictionary of the English Language*," Mrs. Fernley announced, settling herself daintily beside me. "My father's prized possession. He came to this country from Albania when he was fifteen, and spent his whole life working at Southern Steel. However, his real loves were words and learning the English language." Her eyes softened as she touched the gold lettering on the cover. "Imagine it. Year after year of shoveling coal into furnaces hotter than the depths of Hades, and all the while his mind was spinning with the thousands upon thousands of words in this book."

Then she thumped her knuckles against the red binding, startling me. "'Knavery'! See if you can find it."

I slowly opened the cover and began turning the tissue-thin pages, being careful not to bend or rip them. Mrs. Fernley waited patiently while I took several minutes to find the *K*s and drag my finger down the rows of tiny print. I hunched closer. I could barely see in the dim light.

"I've got it," I finally said.

"Read the definition out loud, please."

I was surprised to feel my face burning as I read in a halting voice, "'The character or actions of a knave . . . deceitfulness in dealing . . . roguery, dishonesty, fraud.'"

"Now give me a sentence incorporating the word 'knavery.'"

All at once, I felt angry. What a stupid, old-fashioned punishment. Mrs. Fernley's idea might have worked for kids in the olden days, but for me, it was nothing but a silly waste of time.

"I can't think of a sentence," I said.

"No? Why, I can think of several. What about this one? Miss Gussie Davis committed an act of *knavery* by disguising herself as an escaped kidnapper and practically sending her nearsighted upstairs neighbor into heart failure."

I looked up, searching Mrs. Fernley's powdered face. A little twitch tugged at the corner of her mouth.

"Or what about this one? Let's see. . . . It was a pure act of *knavery* that forced the poor Davis sisters of Myrtle Street out into the hallways of their home desperately searching for their lost underwear."

She laughed before I did. It was a light, rippling laugh, like a stream bubbling out of the ground. And in that fleeting moment, I could see past Mrs. Fernley's tight pin curls, the layers of face powder, and the fancy vocabulary. She was funny underneath it all, and she had a sweet, crooked smile. I couldn't help chuckling along with her.

"Now, I don't mean to make light of this, Gussie," Mrs. Fernley added, her face turning serious again. "I want you to study these words and think about how you can eliminate such traits from your behavior. Agreed?"

"Yes, ma'am." I gave a quick nod and straightened my shoulders. "When would you like me to turn in my assignment?"

Mrs. Fernley rose to her feet. "What about Saturday afternoon at four o'clock? That should give you more than ample time. And you can borrow the Funk and Wag until our lessons are concluded."

"The Funk and what?" I asked.

"The Funk and Wagnalls dictionary. That's what Papa used to call it—the Funk and Wag."

"Oh," I said, frowning down at the enormous book spread across my lap. I flipped toward the back, nearly flinching as I scanned the page numbers. *There were more than 2,500 pages!* "Are you sure, Mrs. Fernley?"

"Of course. I trust you'll take good care of it."

"Yes, ma'am," I said faintly. I slowly reached for the word list on the table. Tucking it between the pages, I shut the dictionary with a loud thump, then gripped the sides of the book and staggered to my feet.

"What's that?" Mrs. Fernley said, squinting down at the carpet beside me.

I turned to see what she was pointing at, and my breath caught in my throat. Miss Grace's folded blue letter had somehow slipped out of the back pocket of my shorts. I had brought it along to the third floor, hoping for some miraculous chance to return it after I was done with Mrs. Fernley.

"Oh, that's mine," I said a little too loudly as I awkwardly lowered the dictionary to the love seat and snatched up the letter. I shoved it down deep in my pocket, smiling. "It's a letter . . . to my Aunt Glo. I keep forgetting to mail it."

I hoisted the dictionary again, and Mrs. Fernley held the door open for me. She didn't look the least bit suspicious. "Now, remember," she said. "No more knavery, my dear. Your poor mother has enough to manage already."

After the door had closed behind me, I stood swaying weakly in the dark hallway for a minute. The close call with the letter had sapped my energy, and now I had Mrs. Fernley's two-ton family heirloom to lug around. I wasn't sure whether I should feel honored or exasperated to be the new caretaker of the so-called Funk and Wag. But I certainly had no desire to go limping downstairs with it just so Margaret could point and laugh at my latest predicament.

I'd have to stow the dictionary in Daddy's office.

He was never around these days, anyway. I paused at Miss Grace's room. The door was shut tight, with a sliver of light shining from underneath. She was home, and it was silly to think she might ever leave her room unlocked when she left for work. Just like Mrs. Fernley, she always locked her door. If only I could slip the letter through the crack and be done with it.

I turned and plodded into Daddy's office across the hall. By the dusky light from the streetlamp outside, I could see well enough to unload the dictionary onto the side of his desk and plop down in his squeaky swivel chair. I pushed off hard with my toe and spun around a few times until I was satisfyingly dizzy. I was facing the windows in the tower when I stopped spinning. Daddy must have forgotten to close them before he left, and I could hear the far-off yowling of two cats fighting in the back alley.

I rolled the chair into the tower and gazed out over the flickering lights of the city. From my perch there was a clear view of the steel mills down in the flats, their smokestacks throbbing with an eerie orange light in the darkening sky. I'd have to ask Mrs. Fernley which factory her Albanian father had slaved away in for so many years, dreaming of words instead of the skyscrapers and railroad tracks his steel might make one day.

I glanced toward Red Mountain and the statue of

Vulcan, and the little hairs on the back of my neck stood up. "Somebody's dead," I whispered. Vulcan's torch, held high in his outstretched arm, glowed with a fiery red light. It was one of those strange traditions in Birmingham. When the neon flame on the torch glowed green, the city was safe. But a red flame meant a recent traffic fatality. Someone had been killed, maybe just a few minutes ago, speeding along on one of the highways that ran like racetracks in and out of the city. And now the light would stay red for the next twenty-four hours.

I felt a fist of worry clenching deep in my chest. *Daddy was on those roads out there.* Just today I had peered over Mother's shoulder at a letter she was writing to Aunt Glo, telling her all about the exciting news. Daddy had been in Macon for a few days, not only organizing his latest deaf congregation but also shopping for the brand-new car that kind Mr. Snider had promised him. "He won't be at the mercy of the L&N Railroad anymore," Mother wrote to her sister. I had tapped Mother's arm and signed, "What if somebody beeps their horn? Daddy won't hear it. And does he even know how to drive?"

"Of course he knows," she had said with a dismissive click of her tongue, as if I had asked the silliest question in the world.

I wheeled back to the desk and snapped on the little lamp, then rolled a sheet of paper in the Smith

Corona. I'd write my own letter to Aunt Glo. Somehow it might make up a little for my lie to Mrs. Fernley. "Dear Aunt G," I tapped out with two fingers,

> *I'm counting the days until we come to Texas*
> *to see you. 58 more to go! Boy, that seems like*
> *a long time. Birmingham and I just don't mix*
> *in the summer. Plus I miss your fried hush*
> *puppies and pineapple upside-down cake and*
> *Mother won't let us go to the public swimming*
> *pool because she thinks we'll get polio and—*

I jumped. Someone was standing in the doorway. "Miss Grace!" I yelped.

I wasn't sure how long she had been there. In the shadows, she looked like a ghost with her luminous blond hair and porcelain skin. She smiled and made the sign for sorry—a quick circle of her fist in front of her heart. "I saw the light and thought maybe Reverend Davis was home," she went on, stepping into the room and talking as she signed to make sure I would understand. I understood just fine. Her voice was high and soft like Mother's, but with the words much less slurred together.

"He's still in Georgia," I signed back. "I'm not sure when he's coming home." I gave a feeble shrug and let my signs drift off.

My palms felt clammy. Miss Grace was watching

me so intently. Did she know? Had she figured out that it was me who had searched through her things? Maybe I had left something out of place.

"What are you working on?" She was pointing at the typewriter.

I flushed and rolled my note to Aunt Glo out of the carriage, then crumpled it into a ball. "Oh, nothing . . . just trying to brush up on my typing," I said, forgetting to sign as I spoke. My mind was racing in circles. I wanted to talk with Miss Grace, to act natural—but my hands felt clumsy and wooden, like bowling pins plunked in my lap. I also knew that if I said much more, I might blurt out everything. *I did it! I broke into your room and stole your love letter! I'm sorry!*

Before I could think of what to do next, Miss Grace smiled again. "I'll let you get back to your work," she said with a sad little wave. Then she was off down the hall.

For a while, I sat perfectly still at Daddy's desk, staring at the spot where Miss Grace had been standing. She looked so lonely. No wonder. Her husband was dead and there was no sign of the mysterious Vincent. Maybe he was dead, too. "My sincerest hope is that you will write again," he had said, but that letter was the final one in the stack. His words tumbled round and round in my head, and suddenly I felt just like that crazy maniac in "The Tell-tale

Heart," the Edgar Allan Poe story we had read in English class last year.

The narrator of the story had murdered an old man, hidden the body in his house, then lost his mind completely when he imagined he could hear his victim's heart still beating underneath the floorboards. And now I could almost feel the letter burning in my pocket, searing through the lining of my shorts into my skin. Frantically I dug out the crumpled note and thrust it deep into Mrs. Fernley's dictionary, somewhere past page one thousand. Then I heaved up the Funk and Wag and set it among the stacks of old church bulletins under the far window in the tower. For good measure, I stacked Daddy's Bible and a phone directory on top.

I switched off the light and hurried from the office. But as I made my way down the dark stairs, I imagined that I could hear the dictionary thumping after me, just waiting for the chance to fling open its telltale pages and reveal my secret hidden inside.

11

**Mortification:
The state of being humbled or
shamed by disappointment or
chagrin; humiliation; vexation.**

Example: Gussie Davis experienced
extreme **mortification** at the thought of
returning to the Advent Sunday school,
especially after claiming in front of the
entire class that the name of her former
church was Saint Delmonico's.

In other words, I couldn't do it. Even after kneeling
in the pew and praying for forgiveness for stealing
Miss Grace's letter, I couldn't make myself walk into
that Sunday-school classroom. My stomach churned
at the thought of seeing Missy DuPage and nosy

Mrs. Walton again. So after watching Nell file dutifully into her class, I walked right past mine, right out the door at the far end of the hall.

I found myself in a pretty ivy-covered courtyard with a trickling fountain in the middle. It would have been nice just to settle on one of the benches under the shady oak tree and bide my time for an hour until Nell was done with her class. But what if the minister or one of the ushers happened to wander through? I carefully opened the wrought-iron gate and slipped out, and suddenly I was back on Twentieth Street, which was almost empty. Church wouldn't be out for another thirty minutes. I watched a young couple pass on the sidewalk in front of me, arm in arm. With no idea where I was headed, I fell in step behind them. They walked quickly and I did, too, peeking nervously over my shoulder.

"What's wrong with breakfast at the Tutwiler?" I heard the man ask his wife.

"It's so expensive, honey," she said. "We better not."

"Oh, c'mon. We deserve it. Our anniversary's in just a week."

The next minute I was following them through the brass-plated set of revolving doors into the fanciest hotel in Birmingham, which happened to be just one block down the street from the Advent. I had always wanted to go inside the Tutwiler, to see what lay beyond the two doormen in spiffy red uniforms who stood on either side of the grand entrance. The couple breezed on toward the restaurant as I stood under the crystal chandeliers in the lobby, wondering what to do next. For a while, I wandered along the edge of the plush Oriental rugs, and even sank down casually on a brocade sofa, pretending that I was waiting for one of the well-dressed people stepping briskly off the elevator.

Then, at one end of the lobby, I spotted the entrance to the hotel drugstore and soda fountain. I headed in and went straight to the news rack, where I knew I could stand and browse through magazines for a bit without attracting too much attention. I was just reaching out for an Archie comic book when someone tapped me on the shoulder. I whipped around to find Grace Homewood peering at me curiously.

"What are *you* doing here?" she signed.

"Oh! I—"

If there's such a thing as stuttering in sign language, I mastered it in the next few minutes. It took me three or four false starts and lots of blushing and hand waving before I came up with a halfway believable explanation for why I was dawdling in the Tutwiler on a Sunday morning. Somewhere along the way, I realized Miss Grace was such a good lip reader, I didn't even need to sign.

So I dropped my hands to my sides and babbled

on. "You see, the streetcar *always* makes me queasy, and I didn't want to get sick right in the middle of Sunday-school class, so I decided to come over here and look for some Alka-Seltzer."

I felt myself turn even redder then. Miss Grace was probably wondering how I could stop to read a comic book if I had such a bad case of nausea. "Mother always gives me ginger ale to settle my stomach," I added. I clutched my middle and pointed dramatically at the soda fountain. "I was just on my way over to get one."

Miss Grace looked a little dizzy from concentrating so hard on my spluttering mouth. Still, she was nodding kindly, her eyebrows drawing together with concern. She led me to the far end of the soda counter. "I'll sit with you," she said. "Just to make sure you're all right."

I nodded back and climbed weakly up on a barstool, suddenly remembering that I didn't have a single cent to pay for ginger ale. All my chores lately had been for punishment, not for earning spending money. This morning Mother had given Nell and me a dime and a nickel each, then watched us seal the coins in our new collection envelopes. I had dropped my envelope into the silver plate just a while ago, relieved that the process had gone so smoothly compared with the week before.

Miss Grace must have noticed my pained expression and thought I was feeling sicker. "Nabs?" she fingerspelled, and pointed to a tray of snacks for sale on the counter. "The streetcar's worse if you have an empty stomach."

I loved those little orange crackers with the peanut butter spread in between, but I shook my head with an embarrassed glance at my pocketbook.

Miss Grace smiled and patted her chest. "I'll pay."

Soon, in a near-perfect speaking voice, she had ordered a ginger ale for me and a cup of coffee for herself. The man behind the counter had obviously waited on her before. He brought a pitcher of cream and two sugars without being asked. I could tell he was smitten with her. When she made the sign for thank you, touching her fingers lightly to her lips, he did the same, beaming proudly like a little boy showing off a new trick.

I thought of Corporal Homewood and the mysterious Vincent. They had probably fallen for Miss Grace the same way, admiring her gentle manners and elegant hands. I unwrapped a straw and took a long, fizzy sip of ginger ale, watching her out of the corner of my eye.

Each passing day this week had helped to ease my worries over the letter hidden in Mrs. Fernley's dictionary up in Daddy's office. I had even managed to complete my first word-list assignment without turning to the page where it was buried. And now relief washed over me as I sat next to Miss Grace. She didn't look as if she suspected anything. In fact, she looked downright happy, munching on a Nab and gazing at the people passing by outside the wide drugstore window.

I touched her arm. "I thought you always spent Sundays with your parents in Mountain Brook."

Her smile faded. All at once Miss Grace was the one blushing for some reason. "Not today," she said. "After this, I need to go to work. I have so much shelving to catch up on at the library."

The Birmingham Public Library was just around the corner from the Advent. We sat quietly for another minute; then Miss Grace turned back to me with a sheepish expression. "You want to know the truth?" she said, making her voice much softer. "I don't have much work to do at the library today. I made up a story so I wouldn't have to go to church with Mother and Father."

I paused, not wanting to seem too nosy. "Don't you like to go with them?" I asked.

"I'd rather go to your father's church."

"Why don't you?"

She heaved a sigh. "My parents want me to go to the church where I grew up . . . where I met my husband. They think I should be with hearing people."

"That's funny," I told her. "I'd rather go to Daddy's

church, too, but he says the same thing. He wants me to be with hearing people."

Miss Grace's blue eyes flashed and she rocked her whole body forward in agreement. "Because you're hearing," she signed firmly. "Makes good sense. But my parents can't understand that I—"

The soda-fountain man looked up from wiping the counter. When Miss Grace noticed him staring, her hands fell still again and she glanced at the clock over the window. "I should be getting to the library," she said, and began rummaging in her purse and setting money on the counter. I had been watching the time, too. I had fifteen minutes, just enough time to sneak back into the parish house through the courtyard and find Nell.

Miss Grace grinned at the empty Nabs wrapper on the counter. "You must be feeling better," she said. Somehow I had managed to eat the last five crackers.

We walked together back toward the Advent and the library. I planned to say goodbye at the courtyard gate, but when I peeked through the wrought-iron rails as we passed, I could see two men still in their choir robes talking by the oak tree. And up ahead, the minister was standing on the church steps with a knot of stragglers from the last service. I almost groaned out loud when I spotted the hunched old usher among them—the one who had escorted Nell and me to our seats in slow motion last week. He stood at the bottom of the stairs, shaking hands with people as they started home.

I clutched Miss Grace's arm, stopping her in the middle of the sidewalk so that she could read my lips.

"What's wrong?" she asked, her face filling with worry.

"Can I see where you work?" I blurted out, edging around so that my back was toward the church. "Can I see the library? I've never been inside the downtown branch."

Miss Grace looked baffled. "Don't you have to go back to Sunday school now?"

"Yes. But Mrs. Walton might be mad if I come in for the last ten minutes of class and interrupt the lesson, and I've always wanted to see inside the library."

She hesitated, wrinkling her brow apologetically. "The library's closed on Sunday mornings. I'm not really supposed to bring anyone in when I work odd hours."

"Just a quick peek," I pleaded.

She started to smile.

"Good!" I signed before she could say anything else. Then I wheeled around and began walking past the church steps, fast, with my head down, as if I was marching against a driving rainstorm. Miss Grace was too polite to stop me and ask why I was acting so strange. She tagged along until we had safely rounded the corner and crossed the street, where I let out a deep breath and waited for her to catch up.

Of course, I didn't really care too much about seeing the downtown library. I just needed a place to wait while the coast cleared in front of the church. Until Miss Grace unlocked a side door and led me down a dark, echoing hall into the main reading room, I assumed one library was just like another.

But I gasped when she flipped on a row of light switches next to the wide doorway. The ceiling was high and vaulted, with gold designs etched on the beams, and all around the huge room, above the bookshelves, were magical scenes painted directly on the walls—a knight on horseback, an exotic woman with gold bangles raising her arms to a flying carpet, an Egyptian king perched on his throne. Miss Grace followed my gaze around the murals.

She had stopped talking out loud in the hushed library, and I had to watch her hands and lips closely to understand. "There are sixteen of them," she signed. "They represent the world's greatest stories." She pointed to a graceful white horse with wings towering over the doorway. I knew it was Pegasus. A Greek hero dressed in a royal blue cape and gold helmet was holding him steady by the bridle.

"My favorite," Miss Grace signed, staring up at the horse. "My mother loved Greek myths. I still remember when I got sick. She used to help me fall asleep by telling me the story of Pegasus flying up to the stars."

I waited for her to look back at me and read my lips. "Is that how you . . ."

My whispered words trailed off, but Miss Grace knew what I was asking. She nodded and gave a little shrug. "I was five. One day I woke up with the measles, and a few days later I woke up and couldn't hear."

I remembered the photograph I had seen in Miss Grace's room—the little girl and her delighted parents before the measles had swept in and changed everything.

I circled my heart with my fist. "I'm sorry," I said awkwardly.

Miss Grace waved away my frown. "Don't be sorry," she signed. She gestured toward the rows and rows of books lining the walls under the murals. "Isn't this a fine place to work?"

"Yes, it's the prettiest room I've ever seen," I signed back, "and so . . . so *quiet*." For a few seconds I stood soaking up the stillness and feeling, for the first time, what it might be like to be deaf. Then, just as quickly, the spell was broken by the sound of the big brass church bell over at the Advent clanging the new hour.

I clapped my hand over my mouth. "I'm late," I

cried. Miss Grace must have been startled when I gripped her in a clumsy hug, made the sign for "Thank you," and ran for the door. I wanted to say more, but there was no time. Nell would be waiting, ready to congratulate me for surviving another dreaded morning of Sunday school at the Advent.

12

It happened the next week, too. I found myself skipping Sunday school again. Yet this time, I went even further. I put my sealed envelope in the silver collection plate, but the offering money was rolled in a tissue at the bottom of my pocketbook. Fifteen cents—just enough to buy a Coke and Nabs and give me an excuse to sit in the Tutwiler drugstore until Sunday school was over and it was time to meet Nell.

What possessed me? I kept asking myself the same question all the way up the block on Twentieth: *How could you, Gussie?* I wouldn't let my mind even venture toward a proper answer. All I knew was that I didn't belong at the Advent. Anything was better than facing Missy DuPage and all the other snooty kids in beady-eyed Mrs. Walton's class—even if it meant keeping my offering money.

At the Tutwiler my pulse raced and my palms

turned clammy as I sipped Coke through a bendy straw, searching the counter for faces I might recognize. At least there was no danger of Miss Grace wandering in. I had seen her drive off to church with her parents earlier that morning. After a while, when no one gave me funny looks or even seemed to notice me sitting at the far end of the counter, my palms dried out and I felt my guilt fizz away like the bubbles in my glass of soda.

By the next week, skipping seemed almost easy. As I munched on my Nabs at the Tutwiler, I even relaxed enough to read the comics and do half of a crossword puzzle in someone's old *Birmingham News*.

Not long after I skipped Sunday school for the fourth time in a row, Daddy arrived on Myrtle Street in the big white Packard donated by Mr. Snider. It wasn't brand-new, like Mr. Snider had promised, but even with the few nicks on the fenders and worn spots of upholstery inside, the car seemed the peak of luxury to Margaret and Nell and me. When Daddy rumbled up the driveway, we all rushed outside to stand on the running boards and take turns sitting behind the huge steering wheel.

Mother seemed charmed, too, as she leaned over to peer at the fancy hood ornament, a graceful chrome swan with outstretched wings. The Packard was supposed to make Daddy's life so much simpler.

And if Daddy's life was simpler, Mother's would be, too.

But as July steamed along, it slowly dawned on all of us that the Packard plan had backfired. Having a car made it easy for Daddy to fit in extra stops between his scheduled preaching visits around the South—a stop at the printing press in Mobile to check on the deaf workers there, a trip to Jasper to perform the marriage ceremony for a couple who were both deaf and blind, a swing through Talladega to visit the Alabama School for the Deaf.

And now, with the summer half gone, Daddy was late again, off on another errand in the Packard, accompanied by yet another visitor from who knew where. And Mother was upset over *another* special meal growing cold.

"Late," she signed. She stood over the dining room table and scowled down at the congealing lunch of salmon croquettes and marshmallow-fruit salad that she had arranged so carefully on her best china a half-hour ago. The ice cubes in our sweaty glasses of tea had melted down to tiny nubs.

"Late! Late! Late!" Mother's rigid hands flew as if she wanted to send sparks shooting from her fingertips. I was glad she couldn't hear the grandfather clock in the foyer grimly striking half-past noon.

With a final look of disgust, Mother shoved her palms down through the air, ordering the three of us to sit. "Eat!" she cried out loud, her voice even higher and more warbly than usual. Then she snatched her apron off the back of the chair and banged through the swinging door into the kitchen.

"Uh-oh," Margaret said with an ominous glance at the still-swinging door.

Nell flinched at the sound of cake tins and a handful of cooking utensils crashing into the sink. "Oh, boy," she murmured.

"Oh, boy is right," I agreed, staring down at my plateful of food. "I guess we'll make things worse if we don't eat all this." I picked up my fork and scooted my salmon croquette around the plate like a hockey puck.

When the doorbell rang and the light bulb on the wall began flashing, I was the first one to scramble off my chair and run for the front door, thrilled at the chance to escape salmon croquettes for a minute. It was Mr. Runion. I pasted on a little smile as I let him in, quickly tucking my right hand behind my back, where it would be safer. Fortunately, Mr. Runion didn't seem to be in the mood for his usual greeting. He looked straight past me and nodded at Mother as she came out from the back hall untying her apron.

Their hands were too fast to follow closely . . . but I could tell it was something about someone from church going to the hospital. "Kidney stones!" Mr. Runion fingerspelled with an agonized frown.

Soon Mother was nodding reassuringly and patting Mr. Runion on the back as he turned to leave. Once he was gone, she leaned against the door and shook her head. I drew a question mark in the air with my finger.

Mother sighed. "It's Mrs. Thorp again," she said in a tired voice, barely lifting her hands to sign. "She's at Hillman Hospital and she needs an interpreter and won't have anyone but your father."

She reached for her purse on the hat stand. "I think he and Mr. Lindermeyer must still be over at Saint Simon's. Who knows what's taking them so long."

"Who's Mr. Lindermeyer?"

"One of the assistant principals at ASD. I don't know what they're doing at Saint Simon's, but somebody's got to go tell Daddy that he's wanted at the hospital."

Mother paused, studying me. Then she signed quickly, "You and Nell go. I'll run over to the hospital and tell Mrs. Thorp that Daddy's on his way. You'll need to catch the number forty and walk the last three blocks over to Dennison Avenue." She pressed some coins into my palm with a warning glance. "And you be careful walking through that neighborhood. Don't stop along the way or talk to anybody, you understand?"

I nodded solemnly, trying to hide my surprise. Saint Simon's was Daddy's mission for the colored deaf over in the poorest section of town, down by the railroad tracks. Nell and I had been there only two or three times, and never without Mother, who always made us wait out front until Daddy was finished instead of taking us inside. Now I could barely believe she was giving us permission to go to Saint Simon's on the bus by ourselves. I shoved the fare money into my pocket and sprinted off to get Nell before she had time to change her mind.

There was no reason for Mother to be worried about us talking to strangers down near the tracks. By the time we got off the bus, the afternoon sun was so hot that the weedy dirt yards and stoops in front of the tiny row houses were empty. We hurried along the cracked sidewalks, hoping Daddy would still be at Saint Simon's. When we passed a block of rundown apartment buildings, all I could hear were the sound of whirring electric fans and a baby's wail drifting through the open windows on the ground floor.

The one person we saw, a wrinkled old man with skin as dark as a Hershey bar, was watering a pot of dusty petunias outside a corner store. He stopped watering as we passed and nodded a slow, polite hello. We nodded back. I knew Nell and I made a funny sight—two white girls in skirts and blouses marching down the sidewalk, pretending to act businesslike, as if we always attended to chores on this side of town.

"Oh, good," I panted as we turned the corner onto Dennison and I spotted the Packard parked down the street. "Daddy's still there."

"You think we should go inside to look for him?" Nell asked.

"Of course," I said lightly, but I stopped at the bottom of the church's narrow wooden steps and looked up. It was silly to be nervous about going inside. Daddy was the head minister for the deaf at Saint Simon's, and the church didn't look much different from any other, just a dark red-brick building with a pretty steeple and tall double doors out front. But I couldn't help feeling as if I was breaking a sacred rule somehow. I was used to white folks and colored folks being separate—separate neighborhoods, separate schools and water fountains and diners, and separate seating sections in buses and theaters. And here I was ready to cross over to what felt like a foreign country, where I didn't belong.

"Come on," I murmured to Nell, and started up the steps. I had my hand on the big brass doorknob when a movement over in the far corner of the entry porch caught my eye. It was a little colored boy sitting cross-legged in the shade of the porch eaves. He stared at Nell and me with his mouth slightly open and his round eyes wide.

"Hello," I said. "We're looking for Reverend Davis. Is he inside?"

The boy shook his head and went back to staring.

"I think he's deaf," Nell whispered behind me.

"Oh." I smiled at the boy and raised my hand off the knob, signing, "Is the minister inside?"

He shook his head again.

"I don't think he understands," whispered Nell.

"All right, then," I said out loud, and waved goodbye. I pointed to the door. "We're just going inside now to get my father. . . . Bye."

With the boy gaping after us, Nell and I stepped into the dim church and let the heavy door creak shut. Then there was silence. Yellow spots danced in front of my eyes, and I strained to see past them. I felt Nell latch on to the back of my blouse.

"There he is," I whispered. Slowly I began to make out Daddy in his collar and black shirtsleeves, standing up front near the altar with another white man, who wore a starched shirt and tie. The man must have been the visitor Mother had fixed lunch for. He was leaning forward, eagerly signing to a colored woman who sat hunched in the front pew. The woman had her back to us, but I could tell she was deaf and that she had been crying. She mopped her eyes with a red handkerchief and rocked slowly back and forth as if to comfort herself.

Obviously, we were interrupting something important. Nell and I both began to edge back into the shadows of the entryway, but Daddy had already noticed us. He squinted in our direction and came striding down the polished center aisle.

"What?" Daddy signed as he came closer. "What's wrong?"

I could see the woman in the front pew turning her dark, tear-stained face toward us.

"I'm sorry, Daddy," I signed quickly. "Mother sent us on the bus to get you. Mrs. Thorp is in the hospital and she's asking for you. It's kidney stones."

Daddy thumped his forehead lightly with the heel of his hand. "Oh, my," he said softly. He thought for a moment, then reached in his pocket for his gold watch.

His face fell when he saw the time. "Lunch," he said sadly.

I traded pained looks with Nell, cringing at the thought of Mother's angry pot-banging. Daddy was too distracted to notice. He hurried back toward the altar to explain and give his apologies; then he led us outside into the humid glare of the afternoon. I was surprised to see the little boy bolt to his feet and scurry over to grab my father's hand.

"This is Abraham," Daddy said with a grin. "But I call him Abe after our great president." He shaped the tall outline of a Lincoln stovepipe hat in the air over Abraham's head. The boy beamed up at Daddy, showing a wide gap in his smile where his two front teeth were missing. Then he reached for the chain leading into Daddy's pocket and pulled until he had my father's gold watch cradled in his hand. I felt a prickle of jealousy creeping over me. From the way Abe popped the lid of the watch open and traced his finger over the engraved design on the case, I could tell he was a special friend of Daddy's. He'd done this lots of times.

While Abe examined the watch, Daddy rested his hand on the boy's curly head and, without signing, said to Nell and me, "That's his mother, Mrs. Johnson, inside talking with my friend from ASD, Mr. Lindermeyer."

"Why was she crying?" I asked.

"Because Mr. Lindermeyer and I think Abe should be sent to school at ASD." Daddy shook his head. "Mrs. Johnson doesn't want to let him go. Her husband's gone and he's her only child, and she thinks seven years old is too young to be sent away to school. She's afraid if she lets him go, she'll never see him again. . . . But he's a smart boy. He needs to go to school—a school for deaf children."

Nell's face filled with pity. "Talladega's not that far. Only a couple of hours, right?"

Daddy watched her lips and nodded. "Abe can come home for Christmas and summer vacation. But that's not much of a comfort to Mrs. Johnson. . . .

She's a lot like my mother. I was twelve before she decided to let me go to ASD."

Daddy gently took his watch from Abe and lifted the boy's chin. He made a few signs—not his usual flurry of hands and fingers, but slow, simple movements that anyone could understand. He tapped his own chest, then pointed to the Packard.

"Can we go with you, Daddy?" I asked.

"No. I need you and Nell to wait for Mr. Lindermeyer and then take him back to our house on the bus. He's staying the night with us."

"Oh, wonderful," I said under my breath as I watched Abe throw his skinny arms around my father's middle.

"You're good girls," Daddy signed to Nell and me before he started down the wooden steps.

I stomped my foot on the porch as we watched him drive away. *Good girls?* Was that all he could say after Nell and I had tromped all the way to the edge of town to fetch him? Plus, I certainly didn't feel like being such a good girl, now that I was stuck down by the train tracks on a day when you could fry eggs on the rails.

Abe must have felt the vibration in the floorboards when I stomped my foot. I knew he was gawking at me again, but when I turned to glare at him, he let out a squeal of laughter. Almost like a high-pitched heehaw. Then he screwed his little face into a giant scowl with the corners of his wide mouth pulled down.

Nell burst out laughing, too. "Look, he's doing an imitation of you, Gussie! He looks just like you. Isn't that cute?"

"*Cute?* You think that's cute?" I didn't care if Abe could read my lips. "Huh," I grunted, and sat down hard on the top step, crossing my arms angrily over my chest.

"Don't worry about her, Abe," Nell said cheerfully, as if he could really understand her. "She's just an old grump." When I peeked over my shoulder, I saw that Nell had pulled a length of string from one of her pockets and soon was showing Abe her full repertoire of cat's cradle—the witch's broom, the cup and saucer, and Jacob's ladder. I turned back to the street, wincing whenever Abe crowed with laughter over a new work of string art appearing between Nell's fingers.

His loud laughter reminded me of Mother's story about going to the theater in the days before movies had sound. Mother said she used to shame her older brother to tears the way she screeched with laughter in the silent pictures. "That was when I didn't know any better," Mother told us. "I couldn't hear myself, so I just assumed no one else could hear me, either."

Finally, the door opened behind us, and Mr. Lindermeyer stepped onto the porch with Mrs. Johnson following close behind. Abe jumped up to greet his mother. She leaned over to fold him in a hug. When Abe caught sight of her swollen eyes so full of sorrow, he reached up to pet her face and made a mewing noise in the back of his throat like a lost kitten.

Even though Mrs. Johnson couldn't hear all the questions in her son's voice, she must have sensed them. "Shush, shush," she soothed, ducking her head in embarrassment. Then, rather than trying to comfort Abe in front of us, she nodded at Mr. Lindermeyer and Nell and me and scooted her son down the church steps. Still clutching his mother's arm, Abe craned his neck to look back as they started down Dennison Avenue. Nell waved until he turned away.

Once they had gone, Mr. Lindermeyer smiled and shook our hands. In my opinion, he looked much too young and handsome to be a principal, even an assistant one. He was tall and slender, with a flop of sandy hair that fell across his forehead. Something about the brightness of his blue eyes gave him a mischievous look, as if he was on the verge of making a joke.

Nell and I introduced ourselves, fingerspelling our names for him.

"Nice names," Mr. Lindermeyer said. He signed as he spoke. Then he showed us his name sign—a letter V touched to his left shoulder. "That's for my first name. I use my last name as little as possible. Lindermeyer. Too many syllables."

"What's your first name?" I asked.

Mr. Lindermeyer spoke clearly. Maybe his speech was a little nasal and slurred like lots of deaf people's, but it was clear enough. Still, I touched my ear as if I hadn't heard correctly the first time.

"Vincent," he repeated. "You can call me Mr. Vincent."

13

How many Vincents could there be in the state of Alabama? Vincents who happened to be deaf. Vincents who happened to work at ASD, where Miss Grace had earned the diploma hanging in her bedroom.

I hoped Mr. Vincent hadn't noticed me studying his every move all the way through dinner. Now Mother was giving me a puzzled look as I joined them in the parlor and pulled a chair next to the davenport where Mr. Vincent was sitting. I supposed she had expected me to disappear upstairs like Margaret and Nell once we finished drying the dishes.

But I couldn't go to bed without seizing every possible chance to learn more about Mr. Vincent's past. My ears pricked up when he and Daddy began to trade stories about their days at ASD. Mr. Vincent was funny. As he signed, he even rose from his seat once or twice to act out the liveliest of his adventures as a student, regaling us with tales of the championship basketball game when he played for the ASD Silent Warriors and of the skunk he and his chum had let loose during the May Day pageant. Mother laughed so hard that her shoulders shook.

I waited impatiently for Mr. Vincent to mention any girlfriends or sweethearts, but he didn't. And of course Mother was too polite to ask him why he didn't have a wedding ring on his finger yet. The grandfather clock struck nine, and I was finally ready to give up my detective work and go to bed when I heard the front door open.

It was Miss Grace, coming home late from the library. As she stepped into the foyer with an armful of books, Daddy hopped up to bring her into the parlor and introduce her to our guest. I stayed rooted to my chair, barely able to hide my excitement as I searched their faces for clues. I'm not sure what I expected. Maybe, I thought, Mr. Vincent's bright blue eyes would well up with tears at the sight of his beloved. Or maybe Miss Grace would freeze in the doorway, so overcome with emotion that she couldn't move.

Yet that wasn't what happened at all. In fact, barely anything happened. Miss Grace might have blushed a little when she fumbled her stack of books into

Daddy's arms so that she could shake our guest's hand. But Mr. Vincent simply smiled cordially, and then there was the dizzying flurry of signs that always happens when more than two or three deaf people get together.

I crossed my arms over my chest in disappointment as Miss Grace said good night and excused herself to go upstairs. Mr. Vincent settled back on the davenport and reached for his coffee on the tray. Then I saw it—the tiniest of clues. As he raised the cup to his lips, I was sure I saw his hand trembling, just enough to make the china cup shiver on the saucer.

It had to be the same Vincent.

By the time I went upstairs, my sisters were already asleep. Whenever guests came, Margaret moved into Nell's bed and Nell moved into mine. Of course Margaret had repositioned the fan to blow in her direction. I promptly turned it back to blow toward my bed, then changed into my nightgown and climbed in with Nell.

I was tempted to poke her awake and tell her everything. Wouldn't she be amazed to find out that Mr. Vincent Lindermeyer, the man sleeping right down the hall in Margaret's room, had once sent Miss Grace dozens of love letters?

"Nell?" I whispered.

There was so much I was itching to pour out. Not

just about stealing the letter from Miss Grace, but about skipping Sunday school. Though if I told Nell about skipping, I'd have to confess that I'd been pocketing my offering money and spending Sunday mornings in the Tutwiler.

"Nell?"

She was lost in sleep. I turned on my side to face her, part of me longing for her to wake up and part of me knowing my secrets had grown too awkward to share. Nell reminded me of one of those cherubs on the front of valentines, the way she always slept with her hands pressed together, tucked sweetly under one cheek.

If she wakes up in the next minute, I promised myself, I'll tell her everything. If she doesn't . . .

I rustled around in the narrow bed, kicking the hot sheet off my feet and rearranging my sticky night-gown. I even began to hum softly—my old favorite, "Beautiful Dreamer," from start to finish. Outside, it had started to rain. I could hear the patter of drops falling against the catalpa leaves.

A minute passed. Then another, until all at once, Nell sighed and turned to face the wall. I turned away, too, and we both settled deeper into our separate halves of the bed.

When Nell stirred the next morning, I rolled over and went back to sleep, grateful to have my rightful amount of bed space restored. By the time I dressed and went downstairs for breakfast, the house was strangely quiet. Mother had left a note for me on the kitchen table. Over a bowl of corn flakes, I managed to decipher her hurried scribbles and figure out everyone's whereabouts: Daddy had already taken Mr. Vincent to the station to catch the bus back to Talladega; Nell was spending the day at a friend's house; and Mother and Margaret had gone to Saint Jude's for choir practice.

I sighed into my bowl of soggy cereal. Our trip to Texas to see Aunt Glo was still three whole weeks away. And with Mr. Vincent gone so quickly, the house seemed even duller than usual. The rain last night had washed away the muggy air, and it was Saturday—a breezy day meant for strolls and bike rides and picnics in the park. But for me, it meant Mrs. Fernley's word-list assignment, which was due at precisely four o'clock. And I hadn't even started defining the first word.

I rinsed my bowl at the sink and stood for a few more moments at the kitchen window, watching the swallows dive in and out of the overgrown grape arbor in the backyard. I had no choice. I'd have to drag myself up to my father's lonely office and get to work with the Funk and Wag.

Then I had a brainstorm—an ingenious idea for a way to finish my word list and escape the house for a while. I rushed back to the kitchen table and carefully added my own note to the end of Mother's:

Dear All,

Went to the downtown library to work on summer reading list for junior high. Be back this afternoon.

XOXO,
Gussie

Ever since vacation had started, Mother had been nagging me about the junior high reading list. She was bound to be thrilled when she came home and found my note.

I flew around the house scrounging for fare money in pockets and under beds, and soon I was settled happily in my favorite spot on the streetcar—halfway back on the driver's side. I pulled my latest word-list assignment from my purse and spread it across my lap. Mrs. Fernley had assigned opera terms this week—a pleasant surprise after the vocabulary she usually chose, which consisted mainly of words to describe my bad habits. The week before, for example, she had picked terms relating to the state in which she found the bathroom whenever she came down to wash her hair—words like "slattern" and "squalid" and "harum-scarum." The week before that, it was words relating to loud, unsisterly behavior, such as "dissension" and "cacophony" and "pandemonium." I had never realized until the word lists began how well Mrs. Fernley could observe us from her lofty perch on the third floor.

I recited the new words in my head. "Libretto . . . nocturne . . . cantata . . . troubador . . ." Finding their meanings would be a perfect excuse to ask for Miss Grace's help at the library. And then maybe I could come up with a way to dig for other answers, too—about her years at ASD, about when she might have met Mr. Vincent.

When I entered the reading room at the library and caught sight of beautiful Pegasus raising his wings over the quiet, sprawling space, I felt the same flutter in my chest that I'd felt the first time Miss Grace showed me the painting. My heart skipped again when I spotted her sitting at a desk near the circulation counter. She was bent over a large book, twirling a strand of her blond hair around one finger.

Her face brightened when she looked up and found me standing over her.

Suddenly, I felt flustered. "Hi there!" I blurted out without even thinking. A librarian stamping books behind the counter shot me a disapproving glare.

Miss Grace waited for her to turn back to her work, then winked and began to sign. "Good thing we know sign language."

I nodded, embarrassed.

"What brings you here on a Saturday morning?" Miss Grace asked, her hands moving quickly.

I laid the creased word list on the desk before her. She scanned the paper, then looked up at me, perplexed. With a glance back at the grumpy librarian, I started to whisper, speaking carefully so my lips would be easy to read.

Miss Grace stopped me with a wag of her finger. "Sign, please."

I lifted my hands awkwardly to sign. "I need to find the . . . the . . ." I didn't know the sign for "definitions," so I had to fingerspell.

Miss Grace was studying the word list again. She made the gesture for music with an added O. "You like opera?"

"Not really," I signed back. "Mrs. Fernley does. She's trying to teach me."

Miss Grace clapped lightly. "So that's the music I feel coming through the back of my closet every weekend!" She shimmied her hands over her desk as if she was feeling the tremble of an earthquake. "I always wondered."

I wanted to laugh, but a couple of people waiting at the circulation desk had turned to stare. I was relieved when Miss Grace led me over to a nearby table and told me to have a seat. Before long, she had brought back not just a thick Webster's dictionary but a whole stack of reference books about music. Then she patted my arm and left so I could get started.

I mournfully surveyed the pile of books, wanting to wail out loud. So much for livening up my Saturday and solving the mystery of Mr. Vincent. For a while, I watched Miss Grace as she worked, admiring how efficiently she helped everyone. I could tell which customers were regulars at the library. They wrote their requests on slips of paper or whispered carefully so she could read their lips. Then, with a quick nod, Miss Grace briskly set off in search of the information they were hunting for.

With a sigh, I hoisted open the Webster's, but the sight of the tiny printed words quivering like germs on the page made me want to slam it shut again. It was impossible to concentrate. I reached for another volume, *The Passion of Opera, A–Z*, and lazily began to flip through the pages. The words "love affair" caught my eye, and soon I found myself reading a description of a famous opera called *Pagliacci*. The next chapter told about *Madame Butterfly*, the opera I had heard Mrs. Fernley play over and over again. I had never realized that Madame Butterfly was actually a poor Japanese girl jilted by an American naval officer.

I turned more pages, and read about the bewitching gypsy girl Carmen, who gallivanted around with soldiers and bullfighters and ended up getting herself stabbed to death.

It was like a cruel trick—the more I read about opera, with all of its tragic stories of love affairs and jealously and betrayal, the more I couldn't help imagining the worst about Miss Grace's past. As usual, my thoughts galloped in crazy directions. What if Miss Grace was like Nedda in *Pagliacci*, who was carrying on with the peasant Silvio behind her husband's back? Nedda wound up getting stabbed just like Carmen.

With so much stabbing going on, I practically yelped out loud when Miss Grace came up behind me and touched me on the shoulder. I stared at the big clock over the doorway in surprise. It was already a quarter past noon. I had managed to work my way through a half-dozen scandals described in *The Passion of Opera, A–Z,* but I hadn't finished a single definition. I slid my elbow over the word list, trying to hide the wide stretches of blank space on my paper.

"Are you finding everything you need?" she signed.

I nodded enthusiastically, hunching even further.

"Want to take a lunch break with me?"

I couldn't help bounding to my feet like a puppy. Miss Grace smiled and collected her purse from her desk. Then she led me through the main library hallway and out into the sunshine of Wilson Park, where a man was selling hot tamales from a pushcart. I had never tried tamales, so I had to pretend I wasn't nervous when Miss Grace bought us two and handed me the steaming bunch of corn husks wrapped in paper. We found a bench under a shady poplar, and I stole glances at her, trying to copy the dainty way she unwrapped the shucks and then ate the cornmeal-and-spicy-meat filling with her fingers.

I was still marveling over how good tamales tasted when Miss Grace wiped her hands on her napkin and signed, "So your father's guest left this morning?"

I stopped chewing and nodded. I never imagined she would be the one to bring him up. And now Miss Grace was touching her shoulder with a letter V—the same name sign Mr. Vincent had shown Nell and me yesterday when we met him in front of Saint Simon's.

"That's what the students used to call him at ASD," she added.

I gulped down the lump of tamale in my throat and tried to look politely surprised. "Oh, I didn't know you knew each other," I fibbed, working to keep my hands steady.

Miss Grace kept her gaze on a couple of pigeons pecking crumbs at our feet as she signed. "He was a few years ahead of me at ASD. After he graduated, he stayed on and taught in the woodworking shop. He was a fine carpenter."

"Daddy says he's an assistant principal now," I told her.

Miss Grace's hands fell still for an instant. "Oh," she breathed. "I didn't know."

All at once, I realized how obviously I had been staring, with my mouth practically hanging open in suspense. I took my last bite of tamale, praying she would go on.

After another minute of thinking, she did. "I'm not surprised he's been promoted," she continued in a burst of signs. "He was a favorite at ASD. When I worked there, I was always a little jealous of how much his students loved him."

"You worked at ASD, too?"

She bobbed her fist up and down for "yes." "After I graduated from the high school there, I worked as a supervisor in the girls' dormitory and helped the secretary in the main office."

"For how long?" I asked in a rush, leaning forward.

"For two years. I loved my job, but my parents had been begging me to move closer to home. So I finally gave in and came back to Birmingham. I met James at church a few weeks later. . . . Mother and Father introduced us."

"You never went back to ASD?"

"No." She smiled wistfully. "James asked me to marry him."

I glanced from her hands to her face and back again, searching for some sort of clue, just as I had last night in the parlor. Sure enough, there it was—

her palms clasped tightly together in the sign for "marry," so sincere and final. Then she was gazing down at the wedding ring on her left hand and twisting the thin gold band around and around on her finger.

I stared at the wedding band, too, my brain racing to fit the pieces of her story together. Mr. Vincent must have fallen in love with Grace when she worked at ASD. But by the time he realized how he felt, he was probably too late. She had married Corporal Homewood, and she was devoted to him. She was devoted to him still, and obviously any spark between Miss Grace and Mr. Vincent had died out long ago.

"I have a new nickname for you," she said out loud, and poked my arm playfully. "Miss Twenty Questions." I could hear the teasing in her voice. Still, I touched my nose and shook my head, apologizing for being so nosy.

Miss Grace waved away my apology. "I like your questions. It's good to have you here to eat lunch with . . . and to sign with. Sometimes I go days without signing."

I couldn't keep my face from breaking into a foolish grin. *Me.* Miss Grace said she liked signing with *me* of all people. I thanked her for the compliment, pleased with how light and graceful my hands suddenly felt moving through the air.

I expected Mrs. Fernley to be disappointed with me. I had finished only half of my word list. But at least she was impressed with the way I used each of those words in a sentence.

"Well, Gussie," she said, looking up from my assignment. "Your work is incomplete, though I admire your use of the word 'aria,' and I quite agree with your assessment."

She recited my sentence out loud in her crispest voice. "'In *Pagliacci*, Canio sings one of the greatest tenor arias in opera history.'" She seemed surprised. "That's very good. When, may I ask, did you have the pleasure of hearing *Pagliacci*?"

"I—um," I stammered, "I guess I never have. I just read about it."

Mrs. Fernley drew back, blinking, as if I had just slapped her hard across the face. "Goodness, child! You can't make such claims in your sentences without at least hearing some of the works you're referring to." She fluttered over to her phonograph and briskly flipped through the albums lined up on a nearby shelf. Then, holding one of her records between her fingertips like a treasure from a museum, she carefully laid it on the turntable and bent closer to place the needle in a precisely chosen spot.

Her skirt and nylon stockings swished as she swept back to join me on the love seat. "Listen," she whispered breathlessly. "This is it. Canio's aria—*Vesti la giubba*. He's just learned of his wife's betrayal."

"You mean Nedda," I added proudly. "Canio stabs her, right?"

Mrs. Fernley nodded and raised a finger to her lips to shush me. She closed her eyes to listen.

I had to admit—even though I couldn't understand a single word—the music was beautiful . . . and sad. Canio's tortured voice poured into the room. First his song drifted off in a sob, and then it began gathering more power, building louder and higher until I found myself digging my fingernails into my palms.

I peeked at Mrs. Fernley. Her eyes were still shut, and she had leaned back in the love seat as if in a swoon. I let out a deep breath, sank against the pink velveteen, and closed my eyes, too, gradually realizing that Mrs. Fernley had the right idea. Listening to opera might be relaxing after all. Compared to the heartache and nastiness those tenors and sopranos sang about, my own troubles seemed downright trifling.

14

Two weeks later, Nell refused to believe me when I announced that Missy DuPage was coming over to spend the night.

"You're lying, Gussie," she cried as I darted around the parlor plumping pillows.

"I'm *not*," I said, gritting my teeth. I swiped a layer of dust off the fireplace mantel with the flat of my hand, then stopped and pulled the damp fabric of my blouse away from my sweaty underarms. "She'll be here in two hours. Now, please go upstairs and clean your side of the room. And if you could just hide all those ratty stuffed animals on the dresser, that would really—"

"But you *hate* Missy DuPage!"

I blew a clump of hair off my forehead and began again, enunciating slowly and carefully this time. "I—do—not—hate—Missy. I told you before. She's nice. We've gotten to be good friends in Sunday school."

Now I truly was lying. The real fact was that I had barely spoken to Missy until a week ago, when she had followed me out to the church courtyard and informed me she was "on to" my "clever little plan." To my utter amazement, instead of tattling, Missy had asked if she could skip Sunday school *with* me. How could I say no? I had no choice but to lead her directly over to the Tutwiler and use my offering money to treat her to some Nabs.

Nell put her hands on her hips. I could swear she was becoming more like Margaret every day.

"How come you never mentioned this wonderful friendship with Missy before?"

"I don't know. I didn't think too much about it, I guess."

Another lie. I hadn't thought of anything else since last Sunday, when I blurted out my spend-the-night invitation to Missy as we were sneaking back into the Advent.

"Did Mother say it was okay?" Nell persisted. "Daddy's having the church vestry meeting here tonight, you know. And some of the ladies are coming along to visit this time."

"Of course Mother says it's okay. And believe me, Missy and I won't go anywhere near the vestry meeting." I rolled my eyes and then swooped over to snatch the yellowed crocheted doilies off the arms of the settee. Nell watched with her mouth open as I shoved them underneath one of the seat cushions.

"You never used to act this nervous when Barbara Blackwell spent the night," she said.

"Well, that's because this is Missy's first time visiting, and I'm sure she's used to things looking a lot more . . . a lot more . . ." My voice trailed off as I stood surveying the parlor one last time before moving on to the dining room. My gaze lit on a bronze statuette that had been planted in the middle of our coffee table for as long as I could remember. I had never understood the statue or why my parents even owned a figurine of a naked boy riding on the back of a bridled turtle.

"Missy's used to things looking a lot more *what?*" Nell demanded.

I grabbed the naked-boy statue from the table and shook it in Nell's face. "A lot more *civilized*," I said loudly, and hurried off in search of a place to hide it.

At five o'clock sharp, the doorbell rang, and I breezed down the staircase in a fresh blouse and pair of shorts, pretending that I hadn't been sitting on the landing for the last fifteen minutes, nervously awaiting Missy's arrival. When I opened the door, I found Mrs. DuPage pressed close to her daughter's side. She was peering over her shoulder at the street, as if she was sizing up the other houses in our neighborhood.

"Hello there!" she cried, whipping around and flashing me a smile that could have come right out of a toothpaste ad. "You must be Gussie. Missy has told me so much about you, dear."

Luckily, she didn't seem to recognize me from that awful morning when I'd dropped my pennies at the Advent.

"*Moth-er,*" Missy drawled in disgust, and impatiently shifted her red patent-leather overnight case from one hand to the other.

"I know, Missy, honey. You're just anxious to run off with your new friend. But, Gussie, dear, I would like the chance to say hello to your mother . . . since we've never laid eyes on each other before. Missy says she'll just ride to church with you tomorrow morning and meet us at the Advent. It's a wonder I haven't run into your mother yet at Sunday coffee hour."

Missy heaved another sigh. Sitting at the counter in the Tutwiler drugstore last week, Missy had questioned me about the absence of my parents at church as skillfully as any of the inspectors in my *True Detective* magazines. Before I knew it, I had babbled out my confession: my parents were deaf and my father was the minister of a deaf congregation and they had sent me to the Advent to worship with hearing people.

"You're kidding!" Missy had exclaimed, and squeezed one of my hands resting on the counter as if we had been friends for years. "How awful," she said, and dropped her voice low, with her look of horror quickly turning to fascination. "You mean they can't hear anything at all? Not even a freight train or . . . one of those . . . those noisy old jackhammer things?"

When I shook my head grimly, Missy's eyes had lit up with delight, and she'd launched into another slew of questions about my "poor deaf parents." But obviously she had decided not to share those stories with her mother for some reason.

Now I was stuck. In my rush to make our house more presentable for Missy's arrival, I had forgotten to make sure my mother would be presentable, too. And at that very minute, she was in our steaming kitchen, up to her elbows in flour and sugar, making a cake and two pies for the church vestry meeting, which would be starting at seven. I had forgotten to tell her exactly what time Missy was coming. Mrs. Fernley's word list popped into my head. *Mortification: Mrs. Olivia Davis would surely experience extreme* mortification *if she was forced in her present condition to meet daisy-fresh Mrs. DuPage.*

Mrs. DuPage was staring at me warily. "Would it be all right, then, dear? To meet your mother?"

"I'm sorry," I said quickly. "She just stepped out . . . to the market. She wanted to make Missy a special dinner."

"Oh, how sweet," Mrs. DuPage crooned. "Well, I could wait a few minutes." She peeked past me into our shadowy foyer. "How long do you think she'll be?"

I hesitated, and we all turned at the sound of a car pulling into our driveway. It was Preston Tucker in a red coupe, bringing Margaret home from an afternoon at the Cahaba River. I had never in all my twelve years been so happy to see my older sister. We watched as Preston hopped out of the car and walked around to open the passenger door for her.

"Isn't that the Tucker boy?" Mrs. DuPage asked, sounding pleasantly surprised and relieved. "The Tuckers live on the next street over from us in Mountain Brook."

"Yes, that's Preston," I said smoothly. "He and my sister Margaret are dating." Of course, "dating" might not have been exactly the right term to describe their relationship. I hadn't seen a trace of Preston since the Birthmark Baines incident back in June. Most likely he was just now recovering from the shock of all the screaming and underwear he had encountered in our upstairs hallway.

Margaret said goodbye to Preston and came swinging up the steps, looking pretty in a flowered sundress over her two-piece. Her cheeks were rosy with sun and the thrill of spending the day with the basketball star of South Glen High.

"Well, hello there," Mrs. DuPage said, reaching out her hand to shake Margaret's. They didn't even need my help with introductions. In no time, they were fawning over each other, gushing about what a fine family the Tuckers were and what a stately colonial they had over in Mountain Brook and what remarkable energy Preston must possess to be able to shoot baskets at the hoop in his driveway until nine o'clock most nights. Mrs. DuPage barely noticed when her daughter kissed her on the cheek and slipped through the front door after me.

Once I had taken Missy to my bedroom to drop off her overnight case, she asked to see the rest of the house. Suddenly, our Oriental rugs looked more threadbare than usual, and I noticed that the rose-patterned wallpaper in the bathroom was peeling away from the corners. When we peeked into Margaret's room, even the flouncy tieback curtains, the same ones I had always coveted, looked dingy and dusty, as if they had never displayed a single shred of flounce.

"You wanna go walk around outside?" I suggested as we stood at the top of the stairs.

"What about your mother and father's room?" Missy asked.

I shrugged. "It's not much," I said, and led her into their bedroom, directly over to the prettiest spot by the window seat.

Missy pointed to the bare light bulb protruding from the wall over my parents' bed. "What's that?"

"Oh, it's connected to the doorbell. When the bell rings, it blinks on and off so they'll know someone's at the door."

"Ahhhh," Missy breathed raptly. Then I showed her their special alarm clock rigged to wake them every morning with a red flashing light instead of a beeping sound. Then the old cowbell that Daddy kept by his bed because he swore he could hear the faintest trace of its special tone. All the things I had taken for granted my whole life, Missy found absolutely fascinating.

"Just think," she mused. "You and your sisters can scream your heads off at each other, and your parents will never even know it."

"That's right." I nodded proudly.

"What about signs for bad words? Do you know any?"

"Oh, sure," I lied. I jerked and slapped and punched my hands through a long series of rude-looking gestures.

Missy watched me with her eyes growing wide. "What does that mean?" she whispered.

"Oh, it's pretty awful, Missy," I said, wincing. "I'm too embarrassed to say it out loud. We hardly know each other."

"Will you teach me later?" she begged.

"Maybe I could," I told her in a forbidding voice. "But you'd have to swear never to make the signs in public. I could get in huge trouble if anybody found out I taught you."

By the time I led her up to the third floor and told her just a tantalizing bit about Miss Grace, the beautiful deaf war widow, Missy was smitten with our entire household on Myrtle Avenue.

"You're so lucky," she said after I pointed out the room belonging to Mrs. Fernley, the eccentric divorcee. "Your house has so much character."

There was more character for Missy to soak up at dinner. Mother had set the table in the stuffy kitchen, since the vestry would be gathering in the dining room in just a half-hour. On any other night, Daddy would have started right in with teaching Missy the manual alphabet or asking her a long list of questions about school and her family, but the upcoming church meeting must have been distracting him. After saying grace and passing around the pork chops and baked apples, he and Mother lost themselves in a discussion of pressing issues at Saint Jude's, with their hands flying and worry flitting over their faces.

Missy watched their every move, barely chewing her pork chop. I couldn't help showing off. I thumped the floor with my foot and waved my hand to get their attention.

"How many will be coming tonight?" I signed flamboyantly.

I could feel Margaret and Nell sending scornful looks in my direction. At dinner, we usually spoke out loud and relied on Mother and Daddy to read our lips.

"Maybe twelve," Mother signed back, eyeing me as if I had lost my mind.

"What kind of desserts did you make for the meeting tonight, Mother?" I went on, increasing my hand speed a couple of more notches.

Even though they must have been suspicious, Mother and Daddy were patient with my showing off. After a few more minutes of watching our conversation, Missy whispered, "Ask them if they want us to serve the refreshments during the meeting. Tell them I'd be happy to help."

I translated for Missy, trying to ignore Nell's jaw dropping lower.

"Well, I declare," Daddy said out loud, and nodded to my new friend. "That would be wonderful. Thank you, Miss DuPage. Thank you very much."

15

Mr. Runion shook Missy's hand hard enough to make the silver charms on her bracelet clink together. She barely had time to compose herself before Mrs. Thorp, freshly recovered from her bout with kidney stones, hobbled over. Then the Tate sisters crowded around, petting Missy's glossy black hair and making the signs for "pretty girl" over and over again. I had forgotten to warn Missy about how affectionate deaf people could be with youngsters. Most of the ones I knew made it a policy to hug you before they even knew your name for certain.

Mother sent me back to the kitchen for more coffee cups before I had a chance to rescue Missy. I brushed past Nell on my way to the cabinet to search for matching saucers. It was her turn to wash up after supper.

"Gussie," she started as soon as I came into the

kitchen, "why were you acting so strange during—"

Missy burst through the swinging door, interrupting her. "Gussie!" she gasped softly. "Are they always like that? What about that one old man? The one who nearly shook my hand off! He keeps grunting when he tries to talk to me."

She made an ugly oinking sound under her breath and then broke out in a peal of laughter. "What am I whispering for?" she cried. "They can't hear a thing!"

Over by the sink, Nell had stopped with a stricken expression on her face, holding a dirty plate in midair. As Missy threw her head back to laugh again and then rushed over to fetch the lemon meringue pie from the sideboard, I gave Nell a withering look, hoping that would stop her from blurting out any kind of reprimand.

"Hurry up with those cups," Missy ordered gleefully. "You can't leave me out there all alone again." She elbowed through the swinging door, and Nell opened her mouth to say something.

"She doesn't mean anything by it," I snapped before she could let out the first word. "She's just not used to deaf people." I lifted up a wobbly stack of cups and saucers and left Nell glaring after me.

For the next fifteen minutes Missy and I shuttled back and forth, taking out the chocolate layer cake and more spoons and cream for the coffee. Every time the door swung shut on the dining room, Missy charged into a new impression of one of Daddy's church members. She was a good mimic, and she hooted and talked loud, reveling in how freely she could do her impersonations of the Tate sisters and Mrs. Thorp and poor potbellied Mr. Hendrickson, all of them quietly assembled just beyond the door, barely five feet away. I knew the feeling. I had done my share of imitations in the past. But this time it felt different, with Nell so full of disapproval, silently rinsing the dishes at the sink. What was I supposed to do? Even though I didn't want to, I peeked at the meeting through the crack in the door and cackled along with Missy, trying to win her over with my own hilarious jokes about Mother and Daddy's friends.

After the meeting that night, once Nell had announced that she was sleeping down the hall with Margaret, Missy and I lay on the twin beds in my room and talked. I must have grown quieter as the evening wore on, because Missy began to chatter more, trying to fill the empty spaces in our conversation.

"Guess what!" she said suddenly, sitting bolt upright and swinging her feet to the floor. "I almost forgot. Guess who's skipping Sunday school with us tomorrow morning.

"Tripp Manning!" she announced before I could reply. She beamed as if she had just presented me with the Pulitzer Prize for Popularity. "Can you believe it? In my opinion, he's the cutest boy at the Advent. I can't imagine how I forgot to tell you. I ran into him last week at the club and told him all about you and your deaf parents and the Tutwiler, and he's dying to come with us."

"You told him about skipping?" I squeaked.

"Don't worry, he won't tell anybody." Missy wriggled back into Nell's pillow and reached over to the dresser for the plate of lemon meringue pie we had sneaked from downstairs. She took a big bite and closed her eyes dreamily. "Mmm. I can't wait. I brought along some money so maybe we can treat for chocolate milk shakes. How much have you got?"

I reached up to rub my temples. I could feel the beginnings of a dull, sickly headache blossoming in the front of my skull. "I'm not sure," I answered weakly. "I'll have to see."

Missy stopped talking long enough to finish off the pie. During the lull, we could hear the strains of Mrs. Fernley's music drifting down through the ceiling. Missy stared upward. "I thought you said your boarder was deaf."

"Miss Grace is the deaf one," I said, my voice dragging with fatigue. "The other one's Mrs. Fernley. She's hearing, and she loves opera, especially *Pagliacci*. . . ." I closed my eyes and mumbled almost to myself, "*Vesti la giubba* . . . something about 'on with the show' in Italian, but I still think it sounds like he's saying 'pass me the goober.'"

Missy shrieked. My eyes flew open and I realized with relief that she was shrieking with laughter. "You kill me, Gussie Davis!" she cried, and shook her head, still giggling. "You are *so* funny. . . . Pass me the goober! You're too much."

It really wasn't that funny, but for some odd reason, I started to giggle, too. Uncontrollably. So hard that no noise came out and tears seeped from the corners of my eyes. And in a minute, I was up on my feet, standing in the middle of my squishy bed, entertaining Missy with my rendition of a very fat, very famous opera star belting out, "Pass me the *goooooooooober. . . .*"

It wasn't until I was at full volume that I remembered I had forgotten to close the bedroom door. I looked up just in time to see a flash of bright kimono silk in the doorway. Then it was gone.

Why? Why did Mrs. Fernley choose that exact moment to pass by my door on her way to the bathroom? Why did it have to be the same day that I had postponed our word-list session because I said I was hosting "a very important guest" that afternoon and evening. *Why?*

I had been on the verge of calling off the next session of skipping Sunday school altogether, but when

Tripp Manning slipped into the church courtyard and broke into a slow, triumphant smile, I changed my mind. Missy was right. He *was* the cutest boy at the Advent, with the nicest wavy hair and the most dazzling brown eyes.

"Why didn't we think of this earlier?" he said to Missy as he joined us under the oak tree where we were huddled waiting for him.

"I don't know," Missy bubbled. She was bouncing on her tiptoes, giddy with excitement. "Why don't you ask Gussie here why she never invited us? She's been at this for weeks."

Tripp studied me for a few seconds, his dark eyes filling with amusement. "Augusta from Saint Delmonico's," he said quietly.

I felt a surge of blood rushing to my face. Missy slapped him lightly on the arm. "Tripp," she scolded, "leave Gussie alone."

I turned and looked over my shoulder, trying to hide my burning cheeks and pretending to check for anyone following us. "We better go before someone comes," I said.

As we started down the sidewalk along Twentieth, Missy began to boast to Tripp about how late we had stayed up the night before. I almost rubbed my tired eyes at the mention of our sleepover but then caught myself. Here I was spending a bright Sunday morning with Missy DuPage and Tripp Manning. If only I could clear my mind of its nagging clutter, such as the fact that Nell had given me the silent treatment on the streetcar that morning and the fact that two extra quarters were lurking at the bottom of my purse. I had swiped them from Daddy's side of the bureau when everyone was eating breakfast, since I knew my offering money would never be enough to pay for chocolate milk shakes at the Tutwiler.

I envied how carefree Missy was—how blissfully she tossed her hair over her shoulders and threw her head back to laugh at Tripp's quiet comments. Halfway to the Tutwiler, she even linked her arm with his, and I looked away toward the street, slightly embarrassed at her boldness. Then I felt a small movement at my side, and to my astonishment, Tripp was offering me his other arm. As casually as I could, I latched my elbow in his and tried to toss my hair fetchingly, just like Missy had a few minutes earlier.

At the hotel drugstore, I was relieved when Missy headed for a booth tucked in the back instead of the soda fountain counter, where we would be in full view. What did it mean that Tripp slid into my side of the booth instead of Missy's? For a brief second, I saw her eyes flare with surprise and disappointment. She recovered quickly, though.

"Three large milk shakes please," she said in her perkiest voice when the waiter came over to take our order.

"At ten o'clock in the morning?" Tripp asked.

"Why not?" Missy said with a devil-may-care lift of her chin. "Gussie and I are treating. Right, Gus?"

I nodded, forcing out a smile. I hadn't imagined she would order *large* milk shakes. And on top of that, no one had ever called me Gus but Nell.

Suddenly, Tripp was turning toward me. "So I hear you can talk with your hands," he said. "Say something."

I shrugged, willing myself not to blush again. "What do you want me to say?"

He ran his fingers through his wavy hair and looked at the ceiling, thinking for a minute. "Say . . . 'Mrs. Walton should have retired from teaching Sunday school five years ago.'"

Missy snickered, and I easily performed Tripp's request, glad to be signing instead of having to think of something clever to say.

Intently he watched my hands sweeping through the air. "Wow," he murmured. "Okay. Do this one. . . . 'Next time we come to the Tutwiler, I want to go in the restaurant and order big, fat T-bone steaks with French-fried potatoes."

"Oh, yum," Missy chirped. "Good idea."

With my confidence building, I signed away, adding a few fake flourishes to dress up my finger-spelling of "T-bone" and "French fries."

"Our milk shakes are here!" Missy sang out when

147

the waiter arrived at our table with three towering glasses filled to their frosty rims.

Tripp barely looked up. "Okay, I got a really good one. How about—"

"Show him some of your dirty words, Gussie," Missy cut in. She pulled the long silver spoon out of her milk shake and licked it slyly. "See, Tripp. Gussie's got us all fooled. She looks real shy and innocent—her daddy's even a minister—but she cusses like a sailor with her hands. Go ahead, Gus, show him."

Tripp turned back to me, his eyebrows raised in surprise. "Yeah," he said. "Show me."

I shook my head and busied myself with unwrapping one of the straws the waiter had brought. I was tempted to give Missy a sharp kick in the shin under the table. Obviously, she was trying to humiliate me in front of Tripp.

"I never cuss on Sundays," I said sweetly, and took a prim sip of my milk shake.

Neither of them laughed. "Oh, c'mon," Tripp begged. He reached out and touched my arm. "Show me. Just this once."

I glanced at Missy. There was a glint in her eyes—a flash of something hard and steely.

I sighed. "Oh, all right." I pushed my milk shake out of the way. I rubbed my hands together briskly. Then, after a deep breath, I barreled into my performance of cussing in made-up sign language.

I knew immediately from Missy's satisfied expression that I must have looked ridiculous, sitting in my church clothes, chopping and swatting and jerking at the empty air. A minute before, my signing for Tripp had felt lovely, like a little ballet of hands. Now it was nothing but ugly and crude. Instead of looking impressed, Tripp just looked embarrassed.

Yet, for some reason, I couldn't stop myself.

"Gussie, stop," Missy hissed.

I kept going, adding a few more jabs and hand slaps for good measure.

"Stop!" she screeched. "Here comes your father!"

My hands jerked to a halt. I peered upward with dread.

She was right—though I barely recognized the person standing over our table at first. This man's face was twisted with emotion, filled with disgust and disappointment as he surveyed the table—the melting milk shakes, Missy and Tripp staring back at him, open-mouthed. His bitter gaze landed on me.

"Give them the money," he rasped.

"The money?" I whispered.

"The money you stole. From the church." Even though his voice wasn't loud, it seemed to rise hoarsely above the calm murmur of the drugstore.

With my hand trembling, I dug blindly to the bottom of my purse until I had all of it in my fist—the two quarters from Daddy's dresser, and a dime and a nickel—the offering money. I laid the coins on the table and shamefully pulled my hand away.

Without a word, Tripp slid awkwardly from the booth to let me pass. Missy stayed in her seat, coolly surveying the scene. There it was again—the old bubble-gum-on-the-shoe look. I didn't stop to apologize or say goodbye as I scrambled to my feet and rushed after Daddy, who was already stalking toward the door. Why bother? I knew that after today, Missy and Tripp would never be associating with the likes of Gussie Davis again.

16

Daddy showed me the giving report from the Church of the Advent as soon as I sat down in the old leather chair in his office. My name was there, typed on the slip of paper—along with a column of zeros, documenting what each of my offering envelopes had contained over the last two months of Sundays.

"Didn't you know the church sends this report every three months?" Daddy asked out loud. "How did you think we wouldn't find out?"

I shook my head, not looking up from the paper clutched in my hands.

"At first, I was sure there was a mistake," my father went on sadly. "I planned to look into it as soon as I had more time. Then Nell told us what she overheard last night."

My head snapped up.

Daddy nodded gravely. "That's right. You and the

DuPage girl were talking in your bedroom about going to the Tutwiler and your little sister had a terrible decision to make: whether to help keep your secret and protect you from being punished, or to tell your mother and me the truth."

I didn't answer.

"I missed services this morning to come find you," Daddy said, his voice cracking with dismay. He *never* missed services.

After that, he fell quiet. No lectures, no parables from the Bible to teach me how wrong I had been. To me, Daddy had always seemed quick to forgive, almost too quick. At Saint Jude's, it was common knowledge that one of the members of the church, Mr. Needham, made a habit of sitting on his front stoop and drinking himself senseless every evening. Yet whenever he saw that good-for-nothing Mr. Needham, Daddy shook his hand and patted him on the back, even *smiled* at him.

So why was Daddy looking at me—his own daughter—that way? With such shock, as if he didn't know me anymore, as if I was already a lost cause, permanently blighted, just like the sickly elm tree in our backyard, with its black-spotted leaves curling on the branches.

"I'm sorry," I said finally, wishing that Daddy could hear the pleading in my voice. I lifted my hands desperately, trying to think of how to explain myself in sign, how to tell him that I didn't belong at the Advent, that I didn't know where I belonged. But Daddy was already shaking his head and turning his swivel chair toward the tower.

The chair screeched as he rose heavily to his feet. He walked over to the windows and stared out in the direction of Vulcan. All at once, I needed to know whether Vulcan's torch was green or red. Somehow maybe it would be a clue to my future. Was I a lost cause? Green or red? Good or bad?

I joined Daddy at the window and squinted into the hazy distance beyond the valley. Red Mountain rippled in the heat. I could just make out Vulcan through the haze, his huge, steely head and out-stretched arm, but I couldn't see the color of his torch. I closed my eyes and pressed my fingertips against my eyelids, which were swollen and sore from all my crying on the ride home in the Packard.

It was when I opened my eyes again that I first noticed that something was different in the tower. The church bulletins, the Bible, and the phone direc-tory had been moved from where I usually piled them on Mrs. Fernley's dictionary under the windows.

I touched Daddy's elbow. "Did you see a diction-ary around here?" I asked. I spread my palms far apart. "A really big one called Funk and Wagnalls? It was right here a few days ago."

He nodded. "Mrs. Fernley came to get it late last

night . . . when I was working in my office after the vestry meeting. She said you had borrowed it. She thought you were finished with it."

"Finished with it?" I repeated mournfully. The words hit me like a punch in the stomach. So Mrs. Fernley had given up on me, too. But who could blame her? I had neglected the last two word lists and mocked one of her most beloved operas in front of my so-called important guest.

I took a step closer to Daddy and carefully laid my head against his chest. I held my breath, praying that he might give in and hug me or stroke my hair like he sometimes did when I was sad. Then I felt his hands on my shoulders as he firmly pushed me away to look him in the eye.

"Augusta," he said, his face still grave. "You'll have to pay the church back for the money you took."

"Oh, I know," I said quickly. "I'll do chores for the rest of the summer and save my money and pay back every penny."

He held up his hand to stop me. "No, that's not enough this time." He hesitated, gathering his thoughts. "I have another way," he began. "The Alabama School for the Deaf is organizing an event . . . a Jubilee . . . to honor the head principal, Miss Emmeline Benton. She's retiring this fall after thirty-five years at ASD. The whole student body is returning early for the celebration, and the superintendent and teachers have asked for my help. I want you to go to Talladega and help, too."

"Really?" I cried, feeling almost dizzy with relief. I couldn't believe it. Daddy was finally going to take me on one of his trips, to a *Jubilee,* no less, even after everything that had happened.

"When?" I signed eagerly.

"Next week."

"Next week? But that's—" I could feel the smile fading from my face. "That's when we leave on the train for Texas to see Aunt Glo and Uncle Henry. Margaret and Nell and me. We've been waiting all summer. Mother already bought the train tickets."

"No, Augusta. You won't be going to Texas this summer."

"But we have to go! It's all planned! What about Margaret and Nell? Aunt Glo's counting on seeing us."

"Your sisters are still going."

Slowly it dawned on me what he was saying. "Daddy, you can't!"

He flicked his hands, shaking off imaginary water—the sign for "finished, done."

I had thought I couldn't cry any more. In the Packard I had sobbed so hard that the tears had slid down my neck into the collar of my blouse. But now a fresh wave of tears came, stinging like acid behind my eyelids.

"You can't!" I screamed, loud enough to make my throat raw, straight into Daddy's stunned face. Then I turned and bolted from his office. I had my answer about Vulcan. On this particular day in August, his torch could be nothing but a blazing, bloody, fire-engine red.

17

The Cussing Woods were the last place I should have chosen to unleash my despair that afternoon. Just as I had during other visits, I pushed my way past the honeysuckle and blackberry brambles toward the clearing. I ripped the leaves off a sweetgum branch, raised my switch high, and opened my mouth to swear at everybody and everything . . . but of course the words died on my lips. Even the thought of cussing brought the ugly scene in the Tutwiler flooding back—how pathetic I must have looked fake-cussing with my hands. I remembered Tripp's handsome face filling with uneasiness, Daddy pale and shaken with anger.

"Give them the money," he had said plainly enough for everyone in the drugstore to hear. "The money you stole."

I let the switch slip from my fingers and sank

down onto a nearby log, wobbly in the knees with shame. What if Daddy made me go back to the Advent? How would I ever show my face at Sunday school again? At least Tripp went to a junior high across town. But there would be no way to avoid Missy once South Glen started in September. She'd be there in the hallways and in my classes, gossiping to her friends about what had happened, about my strange family, about my secret life as a sneak and a thief. I'd have fifty black marks beside my name before the first week of junior high was over.

A mosquito whined next to my ear. Soon dozens were swirling in a cloud around me, frenzied to discover such an unexpected feast in the vacant lot. One landed on my arm, then another and another on my leg. But I fought off the urge to brush them away or slap them flat. Instead, I simply watched their wispy gray bodies swell with blood as they sank their stingers in deeper. I didn't care if it hurt or if I was covered with mosquito bites or if I looked like a gargoyle from crying so hard. What did it matter? I wasn't going to Texas anyway.

I spent the rest of the afternoon in my room. For hours I lay flat on my bed raking my fingernails across my fourteen mosquito bites and watching the shafts of sunlight break through the catalpa leaves and stretch farther and farther across the wall. Just about the time the shafts of light faded, Nell opened the door and came in quietly with a tray of food. I closed my eyes as she came nearer, not because I didn't want to see her, but because I could smell pork chops. Mother must have sliced the leftovers from last night for a sandwich, and now the smell was a sickening reminder of Missy sitting at our kitchen table.

"Mother and I thought you might be hungry," Nell whispered, and set the tray on the dresser.

When I opened my eyes, she was peering down at me. Her face was filled with worry, as if I was on my deathbed, wasting away from something horrible like polio or tuberculosis.

"I'm sorry I told on you, Gus," she said in a small voice. "But I knew Missy was a two-faced double-crosser. I knew she was only gonna get you in trouble. Then I heard her making that plan about the Tutwiler and the milk shakes—"

Nell broke off when I shifted my gaze to the ceiling. I couldn't stand to look in those big doe eyes of hers, so full of sympathy. She thought it had all been Missy's idea. She never imagined that her very own sister could come up with such a nasty scheme.

Nell must have seen the tear leak out and slide down the side of my face toward the pillow. "And I'm sorry about Texas, too," she went on softly. "I don't really want to go without you, but Mother says I have to."

I nodded, and soon I heard the door click shut and she was gone.

Somehow I managed to fall asleep after that. I slept soundly until what seemed like the middle of the night, when an awful realization crept into my dream and jolted me awake.

I sat straight up in bed. "Miss Grace's letter!" I heard myself gasp. I squinted into the darkness, trying to get my bearings. Nell was in her bed across from me. She muttered something in her sleep and flopped over on her stomach.

How could I have forgotten that the Vincent letter was hidden in Mrs. Fernley's dictionary? It had been there all summer, tucked deep in the heart of the Funk and Wag, haunting me whenever I worked on my word lists. But I hadn't used the dictionary for the last two sets of opera words. I had gone to the library to find the definitions and visit Miss Grace instead. And this week I hadn't even bothered looking at my latest vocabulary assignment. All I had thought about was Missy DuPage coming to spend the night.

Reaching past the tray of untouched food, I fumbled for the alarm clock on the dresser and pushed the button to light up the dial. *Only ten forty-five.* Mrs. Fernley might still be awake. I could apologize and ask to borrow her dictionary again before she discovered the letter inside. Quickly I slipped out of bed. I was wearing the dress I had worn to church that morning. I rubbed my hands over the damp wrinkles, trying to smooth them as best as I could.

It was dark and still in the hallway. Mother and Daddy and Margaret must have already gone to bed. I tiptoed past Margaret's room, avoiding the creaky spot in the floorboards, and then crept up the narrow stairs. My arms and legs turned rubbery as soon as I reached the top. Part of me was certain Mrs. Fernley wouldn't be awake, not at nearly eleven o'clock, when she had to buy and sell hats all day tomorrow at Blach's department store. But beaming under her door like a neon sign was a bright crack of light, coaxing me forward.

I sneaked closer and raised my hand to knock, barely rapping my knuckles on the worn wood. The very next instant, the door opened, almost as if she had been waiting for me.

For a minute we stood staring at each other. Mrs. Fernley's hair was set in pin curls, and she was wearing her silk kimono. Without makeup, her face looked naked and full of hollows, lit from behind by the plum-colored glow from her floor lamp. Then I realized I must have looked even stranger, with my wrinkled dress and tangled hair, my red, swollen eyes, and my arms covered in bug bites.

"Yes, Gussie?" she finally said. I had expected that when she spoke, her voice would be cold. Yet it wasn't. It was simply her voice—still prim and proper, but kind.

"I wanted to . . . to apologize," I stammered. I caught myself nervously twisting my fingers together and dropped my hands stiffly to my sides. "For the way I was singing that *Pagliacci* aria last night, and for not turning in my word list yesterday. And I wanted to ask if I could borrow your dictionary again."

Mrs. Fernley raised one hand to her chin as if she was pondering. "I don't think you'll need the Funk and Wag for your next assignment, Gussie," she answered slowly, "or any other dictionary, for that matter."

"My next assignment? But I haven't finished the last one yet."

"Yes, I know," she said. "But I think it's time for us to move on."

"Move on?"

"Just a minute," she said, then went over to her bookshelf. I could see the Funk and Wag, wedged back in its proper place on the bottom shelf. My hopes sank when she didn't bend over to reach for it. Instead, she was returning with just a plain white envelope in her hand.

She held it out to me. "Don't worry about completing the last word list, Gussie. I want you to concentrate all of your energies on this next assignment. You can take as long as you like, and come and see me only when you think you're truly finished defining."

I took the envelope hesitantly, my mind straining to understand what on earth she was talking about. "Are you sure I won't need your dictionary?" I asked again, not even caring anymore about how whiny I must have sounded.

"I'm sure," she said firmly. "Now, it's late, dear. I suggest you wait and look at that assignment in the morning, when you'll be able to think more clearly." She told me good night and closed the door, leaving me in the dark with the mysterious white envelope gleaming up at me.

I *did* wait to open it. For three whole minutes— the time it took me to scamper back downstairs, lock myself in the bathroom, and plunk down on the side of the tub. Something fluttered to my bare feet when I ripped open the flap of the envelope. For a few seconds, I simply stared, too stunned to bend down and pick it up from where it rested against my foot. I recognized the wrinkled blue stationery instantly. I could almost make out Mr. Vincent's scrawled writing between the folds.

My palms broke into a clammy sweat and my face prickled with shame. Mrs. Fernley had found Miss Grace's letter. She must have recognized the faded blue stationery from the day the note dropped out of my pocket in her room when she assigned me my first set of words.

Anxiously, I turned my attention back to the envelope. There was something else inside—something that looked like another word list. I pulled out the familiar sheet of onionskin and unfolded it. This time Mrs. Fernley had typed only one word near the top of the page.

Integrity

What in the dickens did she mean by *that*? "Integrity" seemed like a simple word, especially compared to all the other complicated, tongue-twisting terms Mrs. Fernley had given me over the summer. I wasn't exactly sure of the definition, but I knew it had something to do with being good or honest. Daddy had always admired Bishop Carpenter, one of the church leaders in Alabama. . . . "A man of integrity," he called him.

At last I reached down to retrieve Miss Grace's letter from the bathroom floor. I sat for a while gazing from one to the other—from that glaring word, "integrity," to the folded blue stationery and back to "integrity" again.

Little by little, it began to dawn on me what the painful assignment was that Mrs. Fernley had in mind.

She wanted me to return what I had stolen and confess the truth to Miss Grace. Without that, my definition of integrity would never be complete.

18

I tried to keep myself occupied the next day as Margaret and Nell went about the ritual of dragging their battered suitcases up from the cellar and then filling them with tidy stacks of clothes. Even though Mother invited me to go along, I didn't join them on their excursion downtown to shop for new sandals and bathing suits. Daddy was off again for a quick church conference before our trip to Talladega, so I spent the time upstairs in his office typing out drafts of a confession letter.

Dear Miss Grace:

Enclosed you will find a letter that belongs to you. The story of how this letter came into my possession is a bit too complicated to explain. Please accept my formal apology for not returning your property sooner. You may be assured that such an incident will never happen again.

> Your friend,
> Gussie Davis

Dear Miss Grace,

With deep regret, I am returning an item that I came across in your closet several weeks ago. My intention was only to borrow a pair of shoes for a silly prank. Somehow I ended up with this letter instead. I hope you can find it in your heart to forgive me for this rude invasion of your privacy.

> With kindest regards,
> Augusta Davis

There were at least a dozen more versions, most of which I immediately tore into tiny pieces. Certainly, a written confession was not what Mrs. Fernley had in mind when she assigned me the word "integrity." But as hard as I tried, I couldn't envision myself marching across the hall and telling Miss Grace face-to-face what a vile and devious thing I had done. She would never understand. She would never think of me the same way again. So, for lack of a better plan, I kept typing and ripping until my father's trash can was overflowing with rejected confessions.

I was almost to the bottom of his stack of typing paper on Tuesday morning when Margaret poked her head into the office. "Gussie?" she called over the clacking of the typewriter keys. "Aren't you going to come see us off? We're getting ready to leave."

"I'll wave from here," I told her, barely glancing up from my latest draft. "Tell Nell to look up at the tower before you go."

Margaret rolled her eyes. "You're impossible," she muttered, turning away in exasperation.

"Have a good time without me," I shouted after her. She was already tromping down the steps.

I went back to typing, hoping the clacking of the keys would drown out the miserable little voice in my head that kept crying, "It's not fair! It's not fair!"

But it was no use. I knew I owed Nell a proper goodbye. While Margaret had happily set about her trip preparations as if nothing was out of the ordinary, I could tell that Nell was genuinely sorry I wasn't going with them.

"Who am I gonna ride bikes to the creek with?" she had asked when we were in bed at night. "And what about our breath-holding contests at the swimming pool? Margaret won't do it. She says it'll make her blood vessels burst."

I pushed myself out of the swivel chair and hurried over to the row of rounded windows. Far below, Mr. Hendrickson from church was heaving my sisters' suitcases into the back of his car. He had offered to give them a ride to the train station, since Daddy wouldn't be home till later. Mother was coming down the steps of the front porch with Margaret and Nell, still giving instructions. Even from two stories up, I could read most of her urgent signs. "Wear your gloves. Don't talk to strangers on the train. Don't forget to tell Aunt Glo . . ."

Then, suddenly, Nell was turning and squinting up at the windows where I stood. She shielded her eyes from the bright sun with one hand. It was obvious she couldn't see me through the glare against the glass. Rapunzel—that was who I was. Rapunzel trapped in the tower.

The windows were open only three or four inches. I yanked on the bottom of the closest one, trying to raise the heavy sash through years of chipped paint and grime. But it wouldn't budge, and Mr. Hendrickson had started his engine. Nell was turning away.

My heart was thumping as I banged on the window-pane to get her attention and bent down awkwardly to press my face against the narrow strip of open screen. I yelled as loud as I could. "Bye, Nell!" I cried. "Goodbye!"

She heard me then, and her face brightened as she

whipped around to squint up at the windows again. She waved frantically. "Bye, Gus!" she cried back. "I'll miss you!" She couldn't see me waving just as hard, but it didn't matter. At least I had told her goodbye.

That evening Mother and I ate together at the kitchen table. Canned tomato soup with saltine crackers. We were both quiet through dinner, so quiet that the chiming of the clock in the hall, and even the clinking of our spoons against the bowls seemed to echo through the lonely house. I stole glances at Mother's face, searching to see whether she was still angry about what I had done at the Advent. She had barely mentioned it to me, content to let Daddy handle the matter entirely. More than anything else, she seemed perplexed by my behavior lately, almost afraid to meet my eye, as if she knew she might discover that the old happy-go-lucky Gussie was gone for good.

After dinner, I washed our bowls and spoons, then wandered into the dining room to see what Mother was doing. She was putting together church bulletins at the long table. Even assembling bulletins was better than going upstairs to face the typewriter again, so I sat down to help her fold and staple. I was glad to see a trace of a smile flicker across her face.

For a while we worked in silence. Then Mother sat back in her chair and reached up to rub a sore muscle in her neck. "Have you packed for Talladega?" she asked out loud. "Daddy wants to leave right after lunch tomorrow."

I sighed and shook my head. "Not yet. I will."

I stopped folding and signed, "Have you ever had to do something that you knew was for your own good . . . but more than anything, you didn't want to do it?"

"Sure," Mother said, her hands and face coming alive. "But sometimes those things that you dread turn out better than you ever expected. Sometimes they turn out to be just fine." For emphasis, she made the sign for "fine" again, touching the tip of her thumb to the center of her chest with her fingers outstretched.

"Huh," I grunted. I could tell Mother thought I was asking her advice about my trip to ASD with Daddy. Still, I tried to apply her wisdom to the sense of doom I felt whenever I imagined making my confession to Miss Grace.

"Huh," I said again. There was no possible way that owning up to stealing somebody's love letter could turn out to be "just fine."

"But what if," I started again, "what if deep in your heart you just have a bad feeling about that thing you don't want to do? What if you *know* there's no way it can turn out for the best, even though grownups are telling you different?"

"Well, sometimes you don't have a choice. Sometimes you just have to go through with it and wait to be surprised." She thought for a second, and then her mouth stretched into an odd little smile. "Did I ever tell you what my mother and father did to try to make me hear again?"

"No," I said with an incredulous laugh. Mother hardly ever told me stories about her childhood.

She raised her chin as she signed, her eyes focusing on some far-off place. "I was about your age, maybe twelve or thirteen. Father had read a story in a newspaper about a little deaf boy who went up in an airplane. There was a storm and the plane dropped in the sky—a long way—before the pilot was able to bring it up again."

Mother made an airplane shape with her hand and with a whoosh of breath, quickly dropped it down toward her lap. "Altitude," she spelled out with her fingers.

I nodded, and she went on.

"My father couldn't get over it. The newspaper said that when the plane landed, the little boy could hear. The next thing I knew, my father had hired his own pilot."

I let out a gasp. "He wanted *you* to go up in a plane?"

"That's right. The pilot was based in New Orleans, so we took a train there. My mother and father and me. Then we took a taxicab to the airfield." Her face grew serious.

"You didn't want to go?"

"Oh," she sighed with the corners of her mouth tugging down. "I was terrified. I had never been in an airplane. Few people had in those days. All I could think of was that newspaper story of the storm and the plane dropping out of the sky. All the way to New Orleans, I cried and begged not to go."

"And they still made you?"

She nodded. "My father was determined."

"What happened?"

"We went up. The pilot dropped altitude." Mother clapped her hands to the sides of her head. "My ears! *Oh*, how they hurt! Then the plane came down."

"And?" I asked breathlessly.

She gave a little shrug. "And . . . I was still deaf."

I opened my eyes wide and snorted. "I thought this was supposed to be a story about something that turned out just fine."

"It did turn out fine," Mother said, her voice rising. "Wonderful."

"But how? You were still deaf."

Mother shook her head as if she pitied me for not understanding. "You know Miss Grace's parents?"

I nodded, squirming a little at the mention of her name.

"My father was like them in a way. Until that

plane ride, he couldn't believe that his daughter would never hear. He just wanted to cure me. To make me better."

"And after the plane ride?" I asked.

"After," Mother said, "my father accepted me for what I was." She tapped her fingertips to her ears triumphantly. "Deaf!"

Miss Grace was exactly where I expected to find her at noon the next day—in the park outside the library. She was eating her lunch and reading a newspaper on the bench under the poplar. When I sat down beside her, she looked so happy to see me, I wanted to cry.

"What a nice surprise!" she signed, then pointed to the sandwich wrapped in cellophane in her lap. "I just walked over to the Tutwiler to get this. Would you like half? Or I could get you another tamale. . . ."

"No, thanks," I signed back. "I'm afraid I don't have much time."

That was an understatement. At that very minute, Mother was probably packing Daddy's bag for Talladega, and my father was attending to last-minute details in his office. He still wanted to leave for ASD right after lunch.

Miss Grace touched my knee. "Is anything wrong?" she asked.

I closed my eyes, trying to summon up a sudden

burst of nerve. *Go on,* I told myself. *It's just like Mother's story. Like Mother going up in that airplane.*

"I have to tell you something," I signed.

Her blue eyes clouded over with concern as she watched my hands hang in the air for a few seconds too long. My fingers felt fluttery, like leaves quivering in the wind.

"I took something of yours." I reached into my pocketbook and pulled out the letter. "I took this."

At the sight of the blue paper, Miss Grace jerked as if she had been jabbed by a pin. She took the letter and unfolded it. Her eyes darted across the page, then up at me. "Where did you get this?" she whispered.

"From your closet. Mother has a copy of your key, and I used it to let myself into your room a few weeks ago."

I swallowed hard, blinking back a hot wave of tears. "It was so stupid of me," I rushed on. "I was just looking for a pair of shoes to play a silly trick on Margaret. Then I came across the letters. I only read that one. . . ."

The rest was a jumble. As I rambled on about how wrong I had been and how sorry I was, I kept Mother in my mind, losing altitude, falling through the sky, waiting for the worst.

Once she landed, Mother had said, everything was fine. But already I could tell my landing wouldn't be nearly so smooth. When I finally finished explaining and let my hands fall to my lap, Miss Grace didn't pat me on the arm or say it was okay. She wouldn't even look at me.

"I need to get back to work," she signed stiffly. Then, with her pale skin flushing and her lips pressed into a pinched line, she refolded the letter and stood up to go. She was already hurrying away by the time I noticed she had left her sandwich and the *Birmingham News* on the bench beside me.

A boldfaced headline on the front page of the newspaper snagged my attention. "KIDNAPPER COLLARED IN CAROLINA." They had finally caught him. Hiding in a tenement house in Charleston. Gloomily I studied the grainy photo of Birthmark Baines looking out the back window of a police car.

"This never would have happened in the first place if it wasn't for you," I whispered back at his sullen stare. "I'm glad you're going to jail." Then I crumpled the front page into a messy wad.

I knew I should be heading straight home to meet Daddy, but I stayed in the park for a while longer, throwing bits of Miss Grace's sandwich to the pigeons at my feet. That morning I had gone into Margaret's room to look up the definition of "integrity" in her Webster's—just to make sure I wasn't going to all this trouble for Mrs. Fernley for nothing.

"Uprightness of character and soundness of moral principle," the dictionary said. "An undivided, unbroken state; completeness."

The dictionary was right about the completeness part. So far, integrity felt completely awful.

19

I was surprised when Daddy didn't turn the Packard toward Highway 78 as we started out for Talladega. Instead, he was heading down to the south side of town.

"Where are we going?" I signed as we pulled up to a stoplight.

"To get Abe," Daddy said.

"What?" I cried. "What do you mean?"

But we were moving again, and I had to wait until the next red light for Daddy to answer. "It's good news," he finally explained. "Mrs. Johnson has decided to let Abe enroll in ASD. We're giving him a ride there, and we'll help him get settled."

"But—" I bit my lip and turned away to glower at the shabby row houses lining the corner. Could things get any worse? Miss Grace hated me, and now *this*. But I knew better than to argue. Daddy needed to watch the road. And how typical of my father that this one and only trip with me was actually a mission to help somebody else.

They were in the parking lot at the back of Saint Simon's when we arrived—Abe's mother with her same red handkerchief knotted in her hand, and Abe with a wide grin on his face, waving furiously. Although it was another hot day, Mrs. Johnson had dressed her son in stiff new trousers and a long-sleeved plaid shirt buttoned to his neck. His wiry hair was slicked down, glistening with hair tonic, and a worn canvas duffel bag sat at his feet.

Abe ran up to grab my father's hand as we got out of the car. "Well, I declare," Daddy said out loud. "Don't you look fine?" Daddy hooked his thumbs into imaginary suspenders and struck a dandified pose. Abe squawked with laughter. As soon as he turned to me, though, he scowled and forced his mouth into a fierce frown. I could tell he was mimicking the grumpy expression he had seen on my face the first day we met. He frowned a little more, then burst into his heehaw again and trotted around to the driver's side of the Packard, where Daddy had left the door open.

While Abe slipped behind the wheel and pretended to steer, Mrs. Johnson hurried over to talk to Daddy. She made small, worried noises as she struggled to tell him something important. Her signs were makeshift, half proper and half her own invention. She fingerspelled to fill in the rest. Gradually, I realized what she was trying to say. Abe thought he was only going on a short trip with Daddy, for a visit to see a school for other children just like him. He didn't know he was going to be staying at ASD, away from home and his mother until his first vacation at Christmas.

"If he knows," Mrs. Johnson told my father, "he won't go. He'll be scared." Her dark face filled with fear as she tried to explain.

Daddy seemed concerned, but not as anxious about the situation as I expected him to be. He kept nodding calmly to Mrs. Johnson, and several times he skimmed the edge of his right hand across his left palm, like a boat gliding through water. "It's all right," he was saying. "It's all right. He'll be fine."

I eyed Abe doubtfully. He rammed his fist against the horn in the middle of the Packard's steering wheel, making me jump at the sudden blast of noise. When he saw my surprised reaction, he laughed and honked again, then a few more times for good measure. A woman passing by on the sidewalk shook her head in disapproval.

Oh, brother. What was my father thinking? Obviously, Abe had never been in a car before, never left Birmingham or his mother's side, never attended even a single day of school. How was he supposed to fit in at ASD among all those strange new people and rules and signs he couldn't understand?

But it didn't matter what I thought. Soon Daddy had stowed the lumpy duffel bag in the car and Mrs. Johnson was holding her little boy's face between her hands. She stared for several long seconds, as if she was soaking up his funny grin—missing teeth and all. Then she kissed him hard on his forehead and pushed him toward the back seat, to a spot next to his satchel. She shook her finger and smiled at her son before she shut the door, probably telling him to be a good boy.

Abe didn't wave goodbye. He was too excited about fiddling with the door lock and the handle for rolling his window up and down. It was a good thing he was distracted, because when I turned back to look, Mrs. Johnson was standing in the middle of the gravel parking lot with her face buried in her red handkerchief.

Within five minutes, I realized what a long ride it was going to be to Talladega. Daddy didn't drive faster than thirty-five miles an hour. As we snaked through the scrubby pine forests and rundown farms on the outskirts of town, there was barely enough breeze to blow my sweaty hair off the back of my neck. And cars began to back up behind us on the old two-lane highway heading east, their impatient drivers probably itching for a rare chance to pass on the winding road.

To make matters worse, something smelled. At first I thought it was just a swamp smell rising off the marshes as we neared the Cahaba River. Then I realized the odor was coming from the back seat, from Abe's duffel bag—something mysterious and sour that I couldn't identify. Maybe dirty socks, maybe a musty old stuffed animal that needed tossing . . .

Neither Daddy or Abe seemed to notice. Abe was busy gazing out his half-open window, soaking up the sights. He pointed and laughed and even kicked the back of Daddy's seat whenever he saw something the least bit interesting. A muddy pen full of snuffling hogs, the long drop down from the bridge over the river, a skinny-legged crane fishing in the cattails—all of it tickled him silly.

Daddy ignored the kicking for a while. But after ten minutes of the bumps against his seat growing more lively, he slowly braked and pulled over on the shoulder of the road. A half-dozen cars roared past us.

I was surprised when he turned to me. "Augusta, I want you to get in the back seat with Abe." I felt my mouth dropping open.

Daddy went on, unmoved by my vexation. "Whenever you see something special," he instructed me, "show Abe the sign for it. He needs to start learning. And maybe this will help keep him occupied."

"Jeeeeeeez," I grumbled through my teeth as I heaved myself out of the car and climbed in back next to Abe and his smelly satchel. His brown eyes lit up as Daddy pulled onto the highway again and he realized I was going to be his traveling companion.

I jabbed my finger at a lone cow in a passing field. "Cow," I signed angrily.

Abe let out a guffaw, then copied me. With a big scowl, he held his thumb to his temple and extended his pinky like a cow's horn.

From then on, he would probably think an outraged expression was a basic part of signing, but I didn't care. I frowned harder and pointed at a giant oak in the middle of a pasture. "Tree!" I signed, with my arm held up like a sturdy trunk and my fingers wiggling like leaves.

Abe grimaced back and made his own tree.

"Truck!" "Dog!" "House!" "Man!" "Mailbox!" "Flowers!"

For the next twenty miles, past Leeds and Cook Springs and Chula Vista, past acres of nothing but kudzu, I glared and made angry signs. Abe would have gone on imitating me forever if my father hadn't decided to stop at a roadside station to get gas. Once we were parked next to the pump, a scruffy attendant sauntered over to fill our tank. I sighed with relief as Abe turned away to watch.

But then he was facing me again. "Man!" he signed excitedly. "Man! Man!"

I knew I should smile and congratulate him for being such a quick learner. I could hardly believe he had managed to recall that single sign from all the others I had flung at him. But it was so hot, and I felt sick to my stomach from breathing in the fumes of gasoline along with the nauseating smells from the duffel bag. The most I could do was give Abe a curt nod.

At least Daddy was bringing us two Coca-Colas from the drink machine in front of the station. "How much farther?" I signed when he leaned down to hand our Cokes through my open window. Abe gripped the cold glass bottle with both hands and bounced up and down in his seat.

"About another hour," Daddy said. "But I'm *sleepy*. I didn't get to bed until after midnight. Before we head on, I need to pull over there and close my eyes for a little bit." He waved his hand toward a scraggly grove of cottonwoods at the far corner of the dusty lot. "Just fifteen minutes or so. You can practice signing with Abe."

Daddy didn't wait for me to reply. I gaped at the back of his head in disbelief as he slid into the driver's seat again and maneuvered the Packard into his chosen napping spot.

This was it! The last straw! Margaret and Nell were probably diving into the Cascade Plunge at Aunt Glo's club this very minute. In utter misery, I

flopped my head back against the scratchy uphol-
stered seat. Beside me, Abe was smacking his lips
against the mouth of his soda bottle, taking one
sloppy swig after another. Daddy took off his glasses
and laid them on the dashboard, then wearily
rubbed the bridge of his nose. In five minutes, he
was snoring softly.

I closed my eyes, pretending to sleep, too. If I
could just get through the next hour and fifteen minutes without exploding . . . just an hour and a quarter . . . I could hear Abe beside me rummaging in his
duffel bag: there was an unzipping sound and a rus-
tle of a paper sack, and in the next few seconds, a
fresh wave of that same nauseating, vinegary odor
filled my nostrils. I was afraid to look. I sucked in my
breath and held it.

I felt Abe tap me lightly on the knee. I didn't move
a muscle.

He only tapped harder. Cringing, I opened one
eye. He was holding it out to me proudly—a pickled
hard-boiled egg, glistening and glowing greenish yellow in the sunlight filtering into the car. A slice of
mushy white bread and a slab of ham lay on a
grease-spotted piece of waxed paper in his lap. Mrs.
Johnson must have been worried that her son might
get hungry on the drive to Talladega.

Abe nudged the egg closer to my face, sweetly
offering me the first bite.

"Ugghhh!" I declared, and shrank back until I was wedged against the car door. I squeezed my nostrils shut between two fingers and with all the dramatic flare of a stage actress, cried out, "Peeee-ewwwww!" making sure my mouth was in full view for lip reading.

Abe got the picture. His eyes darkened and his lower lip drooped. Then he bent over his lap, carefully wrapping his pickled egg and his ham sandwich back in the waxed paper. He shoved the parcel in his duffel bag and quietly turned to look out at a bean field shimmering in the distance.

"Ignominy." I still remembered the strange word and its definition from the first list Mrs. Fernley had assigned me. "Disgraceful or dishonorable conduct, quality or action." Clearly, dishonorable conduct was the only way to describe what I had just done to Abe. Wasn't my nonstop ignominy lately the reason I was being punished and sent on this trip in the first place? My parents had realized how mean-spirited and full of ignominy I was. Mrs. Fernley and Miss Grace knew it, and now even silly little Abe knew it. Now maybe he would understand that I didn't want to be his friend or his sign-language teacher or anything else. Now maybe he would leave me alone.

Abe did leave me alone—all during the rest of Daddy's nap and the rest of our drive to Talladega. Even as we rode through the lovely front gates of the Alabama School for the Deaf and past the tall brick buildings with their stately white columns, Abe barely moved. He stared out the window at the towering trees and green stretches of lawn and clusters of signing students, never pointing or kicking the back of Daddy's seat with his feet. . . . Nothing.

As my father cruised along the shady avenues of ASD, giving us our first tour of the campus, I could see him watching Abe in his rearview mirror. Daddy finally pulled to a stop in front of one of the grandest buildings. He fished his gold watch out of his pocket and snapped open the lid, then twisted around in his seat. "Right on time," he signed, and leaned over to dangle the watch in front of Abe's face. Abe didn't reach for it. He didn't even crack a smile, just kept blinking up at those massive columns and the formal wrought-iron balcony running the length of the building's second floor.

After studying him thoughtfully for a minute, Daddy turned to put his watch away and then followed Abe's gaze to the curlicued tops of the columns. He sighed. "I was just as scared when I first saw Manning Hall," he said. His voice was faint and wispy. I hung over the front seat so that I could hear.

"I still remember my mother walking me through those front doors when we came to enroll," he went on. "They looked so big to me then. We met the principal and my mother made me shake his hand." He let out a chuckle. "We had just gotten a new puppy before I left home. He was furry all over. When I shook that principal's hand and saw how hairy his wrist was, I pointed and said, 'Puppy.'"

Daddy's shoulders shook as he laughed over the memory. "My mother was *so* humiliated. She had been working with me on my speaking voice, trying to get me to talk more clearly. 'Puppy' was a word I could always say perfectly."

Some sort of foolish instinct made me glance back to see if Abe was laughing along with us. But of course he was only gawking in bewilderment.

"We better get him checked in," Daddy said, adjusting his glasses and reaching for the key in the ignition.

I touched him on the elbow. "I thought you said new students check in here, at Manning Hall."

"Not the colored students," he told me. "They have a separate school over on Fort Lashley Avenue."

Daddy started the car then, and we rode back through the fancy gates, over a set of railroad tracks, and along a country road. It was no surprise to me that the colored school and the white school were separate, but I never imagined that two or three miles of pastureland and pine thickets would divide them. The farther we drove, the guiltier I began to feel about how I had treated Abe. I sneaked another look at him. He was still pressed into the corner, staring out the window in a daze.

20

There was no gate or sign to mark the Alabama School for the Negro Deaf—just a long, straight gravel driveway leading to a collection of official-looking brick buildings planted oddly among the flat spread of farm fields. While the main campus had been bustling, there wasn't a soul around the colored school. It was so quiet when Daddy turned off the engine, I could hear a flock of blackbirds fussing in a far-off treetop.

Daddy and I climbed from the car, stretching our cramped muscles. Abe didn't get out behind us. He stayed rooted to his spot in the sweltering back seat until Daddy opened the door and coaxed him out with a beckoning hand.

"Come," he signed cheerfully. "Come and see!"

"Where is everybody?" I asked once the three of us were standing on the walkway facing a large center building flanked by two matching smaller ones. Rows of blank windows yawned back at us.

"The students and teachers here won't arrive for another few days, after Miss Benton's retirement celebration is over."

I lifted my hand to ask what Abe was supposed to do until then, but Daddy was already leading us over to admire the sturdy construction of the boys' dormitory. He pointed out the fine brickwork and stone trim, then knocked his fist against the closest brick and made a show of flexing his biceps. "Strong," he signed to Abe. "Like you."

Daddy turned to me. "He's lucky," he told me. "This is all brand-new, finished about a year ago. Fireproofed and steam heated. Until now, all the Negroes—both blind and deaf—used to be crowded together in the old institution over on MacFarland, sometimes two or three to a bunk."

I pressed my face against a windowpane in the dormitory door, trying to peer past the dim foyer and imagine Abe spending the next ten years of his life there. But all I could see was a mop propped in an old scrub bucket and a forgotten pair of galoshes. "It's locked," I told Daddy.

He nodded. "Let's go see if we can find the principal." Abe clung to my father's side as we made our way back to the main building and through the front door. The school office was empty, but I could hear the sound of hammering echoing through the halls.

"Someone's here," I signed to Daddy, and touched my ear. "I can hear them. Follow me."

I scurried ahead along the shadowy corridor, glad to be in the lead for a change. I peeked into one empty classroom after another, hunting for the source of the banging. It wasn't until I stuck my head into the last room on the right that I spotted a man in work clothes crouching over an upturned desk.

"Excuse me," I called from the doorway. When the man didn't lift his head, I realized he was probably deaf, so I took a few steps closer and stomped on the hardwood floor, hoping not to startle him. That very second, he sprang upright, the hammer raised like a weapon in his hand.

We both gasped at the same time.

"Mr. Vincent!" I cried, feeling myself touch the letter *V* to my shoulder.

"Sorry," he said out loud, and set the hammer down on a nearby desk. He blew out a heavy whoosh of air. "You scared me."

"What are you doing here?" I asked.

I hadn't meant to be so blunt, but Mr. Vincent was kind enough to overlook any rudeness as he read my lips. "Well," he said, chuckling and glancing down at his rolled-up shirtsleeves and worn trousers. "You wouldn't know it to look at me, but I'm the principal here. I never thought my old carpentry days would come in so handy." He glanced around the room at the rows of old desks. "Every single one of these needs fixing."

"You're the principal here?" I repeated lamely. My hodgepodge of knowledge about Mr. Vincent Lindermeyer came tumbling back. I remembered Miss Grace telling me, as we ate tamales in the park, that he had taught carpentry, that all his students loved him. I blushed, suddenly recalling the stolen note. "Our letters are the last tie binding us together," it had said . . . and there was no doubt I had seen that coffee cup tremble in his hand right after Miss Grace appeared unexpectedly in our parlor.

Stop it! I told myself. *Your days of poking into other people's business are over.* Integrity. *Remember?*

With clumsy fingers, I began to sign. "I knew you were an assistant principal at ASD, I just didn't know you worked at the—"

"At the Negro school?" Mr. Vincent offered.

I nodded.

"It just happened last month. The old principal left, and the superintendent gave me the job."

I was grateful to see Daddy and Abe appear in the doorway. Mr. Vincent hurried forward to greet them, happily flinging out their name signs. "Reverend Davis! And my good friend Abraham!"

For the first time in two hours a hint of a smile

slipped across Abe's face. Over his head, my father and Mr. Vincent exchanged a whirlwind of signs. I managed to decipher most of them.

"Thank you for bringing him," Mr. Vincent said.

"He doesn't know," Daddy told him, "that he's here to stay."

Mr. Vincent tapped his chin thoughtfully. "I'll take my time telling him. One of our cooks is coming back early to help keep an eye on him over the next few days. He'll spend the nights with him in the dormitory. Until the others come."

"Fine," Daddy signed. "Good."

We wandered back toward the front entrance, stopping for Mr. Vincent to show off a few sights along the way—the barely used set of encyclopedias someone had donated to the tiny library, the home economics room with its electric stove and gleaming pair of sewing machines waiting to be fired into action. Daddy and Mr. Vincent spoke so casually that I knew poor Abe had no idea of what was about to occur. It wasn't until we were outside again, standing on the front walkway, when Mr. Vincent wrapped his arm protectively around the boy's shoulder, that Abe realized for certain something was wrong. Daddy gently asked me to fetch Abe's things from the car, and when I came back holding the duffel bag, I saw Abe's narrow shoulders stiffen. He looked up at my father, frantically searching his face for clues.

A fresh flood of guilt washed over me. If it could have made Abe feel any better, I would have rummaged down in the duffel bag for the greasy waxed-paper package, pulled out the pickled egg, and taken a giant bite.

"Delicious," I would have declared, patting my stomach and smiling to make him understand . . . anything to prove how sorry I was. But all I managed to do was press the worn bag into Abe's hands and hurry back to the car. I couldn't look at his small confused face anymore, crumpling as Daddy told him goodbye.

21

All around me deaf kids were clapping. A few of the boys even waved their white handkerchiefs as my father strode to the center of the stage to welcome the students of ASD back from their summer vacation.

I folded my arms across my chest and slouched in my seat among all the intermediate-department girls in the fifth row of the auditorium. Daddy had been so busy since our arrival, I had barely laid eyes on him after he dropped me off at the girls' dormitory the night before. Who could blame me for being put out? My father had left me stranded like a castaway on Deaf Island.

I glared and chewed my fingernails, watching half-heartedly as he signed his thanks to everyone for returning early to celebrate the stupendous accomplishments of the great Miss Emmeline Benton.

Hmmph, another person I hadn't seen a trace of since I arrived at ASD.

"You may find this difficult to believe," Daddy signed, "but Miss Benton was here when I was a student at ASD. She was a teacher then, and I will never forget her firm but loving ways. I cannot imagine devoting our minds and hearts to a finer task than honoring this woman, who has dedicated her life to helping others."

Next, Daddy led the audience in a prayer asking God to watch over the hundreds of students Miss Benton had taught over so many years. But just as he signed "Amen" and seemed ready to turn the stage over to the superintendent of the school, a commotion broke out in the back of the assembly hall. When I turned around, I saw one of the older boys leap up with a folded piece of paper in his hand. His grinning friends pushed him out to the aisle, and he trotted down to the foot of the stage and handed the note up to my father.

Before Daddy even finished reading it, the superintendent had rushed over to investigate. As they both scanned the note, I could see Daddy working to hold back a playful smile. The superintendent, on the other hand, didn't seem quite so amused. Like most of the teachers and dormitory monitors at ASD, he was hearing. But I could see how much he respected Daddy by the way he consulted with him up on the stage. He turned and spoke carefully so it would be easier for my father to read his lips. And when the boys in the back started waving their handkerchiefs again, the superintendent scowled out at them until Daddy patted his arm and reassured him with a few soothing words. With that, the man finally gave a resigned nod and went to stand behind the curtain at the edge of the stage.

I found myself leaning forward along with everyone else as my father lifted his hands for an announcement. "I have had a request from the young men of the advanced department," Daddy signed grandly. "With kind permission from your superintendent, I am happy to begin where we left off during my last visit and present another installment of Mr. Victor Hugo's *The Hunchback of Notre Dame*."

"What?" I whispered to myself, but the audience had already burst into another round of hanky waving and loud applause. A few kids hooted and stomped with enthusiasm. Obviously, Daddy's dramatic performances had become a tradition at the school. Within seconds, someone had darkened the hall and trained a single spotlight on Daddy until he seemed to glow at the center of the stage.

I could hardly believe that was my father up there. I had heard people compliment the way he borrowed interesting stories from books or his own life to work into his sermons, but this was something else. With graceful and swooping signs he began to tell the tale of a poor hunchback named Quasimodo, who was a bell ringer in the most famous cathedral in Paris. "He was deaf, like all of us," Daddy signed. "So deaf that he couldn't hear the thundering chime of his own cathedral bells."

One minute Daddy was Quasimodo, limping back and forth with his deformed shoulder, regaling us with his lovesick descriptions of a beautiful gypsy dancer named Esmeralda. The next minute, he turned into an evil archdeacon, sentencing Esmeralda to hang for a crime she didn't commit.

I peered through the darkness in amazement at the rows of deaf children seated around me. For the first time since I had come to ASD, the whole restless crowd of them was perfectly still—hands at rest, all eyes riveted to the hunched figure on the stage who had just rescued Esmeralda from the brink of death and carried her back to the bell tower to hide from the guards.

Soon even I was lost in the story . . . until my trance was broken by the sound of someone sniffling beside me. It was Belinda Bates, a girl with bright, carrot-colored hair tied into braids. The night before, she had shyly approached me in the dormitory bathroom and spelled out her name and where she was from. Pickens, Alabama. Now I watched Belinda bite her lip and heave a shuddering sigh as Daddy finally revealed the hunchback's tragic fate—to die of heart-break, his love for the beautiful gypsy dancer never returned.

When he was finished, my father bowed low and smiled out at the sea of clapping hands. Slowly I raised my own hands to join in the applause. Despite being frustrated with Daddy, I couldn't help being proud, too. The girls in my row, even some high-school-aged ones across the aisle, had nudged their friends and turned to stare. Word had spread. "That's the Reverend's daughter," I saw one of them say with a quick flash of hands.

After a speech from the superintendent, signed by a deaf teacher, everyone was dismissed for the evening. As we all filed toward the exit, I craned my neck, trying to catch sight of Daddy. I was itching to search him out and ask if we could have breakfast together in the dining hall the next morning, so I wouldn't have to spend another mealtime surrounded by dozens of deaf girls too bashful to include me in their conversations.

But before I could slip away, Miss Hinkle, one of the dormitory supervisors, spotted me. Miss Hinkle was a brisk, no-nonsense sort of woman who had assigned me a bed on the second floor of Graves Hall and issued me a set of sheets with a blanket and a pillow. This morning she had woken the girls in her section—unfortunately, including me—at six a.m. by rudely flashing the overhead lights on and off. And all that day, she never seemed to be without her clipboard, scribbling notes as she stalked, sharp-eyed, between the beds and along the echoing hallways of ASD. Tonight she had the same clipboard tucked firmly under her arm.

"There you are, Miss Davis," she said, pushing her way in beside me as we crowded up the aisle.

"You can call me Gussie," I told her.

She barked out a dry little laugh. "I would never dream of addressing the daughter of Reverend Davis by her first name. As you must have noticed earlier tonight, your father's a very important person around here. His performances are quite the favorite among the students. . . . I thought I'd never get them calmed down after his rendition of 'Casey at the Bat' last year."

I stayed quiet, perplexed by the strange tone in her voice, and she went on crisply. "Besides, you've been so kind to accompany your father and help our intermediate girls get ready for the Jubilee on Saturday. It's only fitting that we should call you Miss Davis—just as if you were a teacher here."

"All right," I said, feeling silly. I was barely a year older than the group of girls I was supposed to be supervising. "I'm afraid I wasn't much help during the first rehearsal this morning," I added sheepishly.

"Well, they always have a hard time following

directions after being away for the summer. With any luck, they'll be ready for instruction tomorrow."

I tried not to cringe. I didn't like the icy way she kept referring to the girls as "they." Plus, that morning's practice had been a disaster from the moment Miss Hinkle announced that the students under her charge would be performing a Maypole dance for the Jubilee.

"A Maypole dance in August?" I had blurted out in front of all the girls.

That was when Miss Hinkle had explained to me, rather impatiently, that the dance would be in recognition of the fine May Day pageants Miss Benton had organized so devotedly each of her thirty-five springs at ASD.

"Oh," I had replied.

But I could see the girls' faces turning bleak, their shoulders drooping, as Miss Hinkle marched all thirteen of us out to the wide front lawn, where the Maypole stood ready.

"See?" Miss Hinkle had noted proudly, snipping the twine binding the ribbons against the pole. "I've chosen the school colors." As we all watched the red and gold streamers drift upward in the breeze, a girl next to me had let out a tiny moan. It didn't take long to understand why: dancing around a Maypole is a lot trickier than it looks. And to make matters worse, Miss Hinkle didn't know a lick of sign language.

After squinting down at the notes on her clipboard for a long moment, she had grasped each girl by the shoulders and pushed them into position, some facing one way, some facing another. Then she had charged around the pole, pressing ribbons into hands, pointing this way and that, and mouthing directions until we were all muddled with confusion.

"You need to weave," she kept enunciating into the girls' blank faces. "In and out. Over and under. Weeeeeeave. . . ."

I had tried to help. I dove under the canopy of ribbons and steered girls over and under, back and forth, wherever I thought Miss Hinkle meant for them to go. But in seconds we were in a hopeless tangle of arms and legs and streamers. I was glad no one else could hear Miss Hinkle shouting, "Stop! Stop! Stop!"

But the fiasco of our first practice wasn't enough to make Miss Hinkle abandon her idea. As we filed out of the auditorium after the assembly, she said, "Don't worry, Miss Davis. I'll have you review the weaving patterns before you go out to rehearse in the morning with the girls. Did your father tell you? You'll be in charge."

I almost stumbled over the girl in front of me. "In charge?" I squeaked. "He didn't tell me about being in charge."

"Well, maybe he wasn't aware of it. But many of Miss Benton's former students begin arriving tomorrow. Everything has changed so much since they were here at ASD. The superintendent needs someone to lead the alumni on tours of the school." She gave a haughty sniff. "I was the only dormitory supervisor selected for the duty."

"But, Miss Hinkle, I don't know anything about Maypole dancing."

"Oh, you seem like a smart girl," she breezed on. "You'll do fine."

I swallowed. "When did you say we need to be ready?"

"The program starts at one o'clock on Saturday. Ours will actually be the first performance, since we'll need to remove the Maypole after we're done, to make room for the other numbers."

I felt my face freeze into a sickly smile. Saturday was the day after tomorrow. *Dang it*. What had Daddy gotten me into?

We stepped into the warm August night. Out on the lawn a firefly flickered, reminding me of catching swarms of them in Mason jars at Aunt Glo's. I looked down at my wristwatch. Eight-thirty. If I was in Texas, I'd be settling down to homemade peach ice cream on Aunt Glo's porch right about now, or maybe sliding down for a soak in her old clawfoot tub. . . .

Miss Hinkle and I walked in silence the rest of the way back to the girls' dormitory. By the time we reached the second floor of Graves Hall, I was so lost in longing for Texas that I jumped when I heard Miss Hinkle speak out suddenly in a sharp voice.

"Just look at that," she snapped, stopping on the edge of the vast sprawl of beds.

I blinked. "Look at what?" There wasn't anything unusual that I could see—just some girls pulling off their shoes, getting ready for bed. Another group had gathered in the corner, signing excitedly and giggling.

"*That,*" she said with disgust, stabbing her finger toward the cluster of girls. "That talking on their hands. No matter how much I scold them, they still persist."

"What do you mean?" I asked, completely baffled. "How else are they supposed to talk with each other?"

She looked shocked that I had even asked such a question. "Speaking and lip reading, of course," she said. Her voice hardened with determination. "They'll never be able to get along in the hearing world if they don't learn those oral skills properly. And how are they supposed to learn if they insist on doing nothing but that hand talk whenever I turn my back?"

I stared with my mouth open as Miss Hinkle threaded her way between the beds like a cat, with stealthy steps, every muscle poised to pounce. At the sight of the dorm supervisor bearing down on them, two of the girls stopped cold, the smiles evaporating from their faces. But the poor red-haired girl, Belinda Bates, was facing the other direction, still happily signing away when Miss Hinkle shoved into their circle and snatched Belinda's hand out of the air.

She leaned into the cringing girl's face and spat her syllables out slowly. "I—told—you—to—talk—with—your—lips—not—your—hands!" With each exaggerated word, she slapped her clipboard against her thigh. Then she flung Belinda's wrist away and whirled around to the other girls, pointing to her own mouth. "Like this. See? *Like this!*"

Once all three of them had dutifully said the words "Yes, ma'am" out loud, Miss Hinkle ordered them to get ready for bed. Then she stalked off to her own small quarters at the far end of the room, yanking the door shut behind her. For a while, I stood motionless, shaken with anger and the unfairness of it all. Poor Belinda. I could see her rubbing her sore wrist as she solemnly began to undo her braids for the night. I expected her to burst into tears at any second. But instead, to my surprise, she broke into a throaty laugh when one of her friends slipped closer and furtively signed something else about "mean old Miss Wrinkle." I couldn't help smiling myself. Hinkle. Wrinkle. Pretty clever.

Then something strange happened. Belinda and

her friend must have spied me watching, because all at once they fell still again and looked back at me with wary expressions. As they quickly moved apart, a wave of astonishment rippled through me. They actually thought I *agreed* with Miss Hinkle, that I believed signing was an oddity, something to be ashamed of or hidden away.

I made my way over to my bed and sank down on the narrow mattress feeling lonelier and more cut off from Daddy's world than ever. Of course, I knew it was my own fault. So far I had barely even bothered to talk *or* sign with any of the other girls at ASD. And what about how I had treated Abe when he needed my help the most? No wonder Belinda and her friends assumed I was just like all the other Ears.

A few minutes after I changed into my nightgown, Miss Hinkle reappeared and marched through the rows of beds. Like the previous night, the girls knew it was time to drop to their knees on the hardwood floor and press their palms together for the nightly prayer. They watched Miss Hinkle's lips and followed along as best they could while she stood over them reciting the prayer in a flat, droning voice. There was barely time to say "Amen" before she announced, "Lights out!" and flipped the switch to darken our section of the dormitory.

Soon the entire second floor was as dark as a coal cellar. I stayed awake for what seemed like ages, still confused and miserable, listening to the night noises of the dormitory that no one else around me could hear. Someone was snoring over in the corner, and the crickets had set to chirping outside. But then I heard the soft creak of bedsprings and feet padding across the floor. I sat up in bed just in time to see three shadowy figures scampering along the wall of windows toward the hallway.

I couldn't bear not to follow them. They were in the bathroom—Belinda and two other girls, the same ones Miss Hinkle had scolded earlier. I didn't see them at first. They had hidden in the shower room, in the last big stall on the left. I could hear them laughing, but when I peeked around the edge of the shower curtain, they all jumped, their hands flying to their mouths in surprise.

"It's all right!" I signed, pushing the curtain aside. "I won't tell!"

Belinda's freckles stood out like orange paint splashed on her pale skin. She spoke out loud in a high, thin voice. "We were just . . . we just come here to talk sometimes after lights out."

"You can sign all you want with me," I rushed to tell her. My hands had taken on a life of their own. "Miss Hinkle has no right. No right to make you stop signing. I think signing is . . . is wonderful!"

The girls gawked at me, startled even more by my sudden outburst.

"Are they all that bad?" I hurried on. "The dorm supervisors? Are they all as strict as Miss Wrinkle?" I signed the word "wrinkle" with a dose of theatrics, twisting my face into a grimace and dragging my fingernails down my cheeks like claws.

They broke into nervous smiles then, and Belinda shook her head. "Miss Hinkle's the worst. She's the only supervisor who cares if we sign during our free time. All the others let their girls sign in the dining hall or in the dorm. But Miss Hinkle thinks she's a teacher, for some reason. Maybe because she's been here so long."

"The teachers don't allow signing in class?" I asked in amazement. "Never?"

The tall, tomboyish girl named Hattie shook her head. "Never. I got my hands smacked with a ruler three times last year for signing in composition class."

"How do you learn, then, if they don't sign?"

Hattie shrugged. "Books. Blackboard. Reading lips. . . . But it's hard sometimes," she added, furrowing her brow.

It didn't take long before we were all sitting on the wooden benches lining one end of the shower room. They wanted to tell me everything, about how impossible it was to read Mr. Carney's lips in math class. He was a mumbler. And Mrs. Devon, the sewing teacher, was even harder to understand, with her big overbite. We all collapsed into snorts of laughter as Belinda did her imitation of Mrs. Devon, pushing out her front teeth like a crazed rabbit.

Then Hattie told about her first day at ASD. "I had never seen anyone signing before," she told me. "Back home I had always just looked at people's lips to get by. When I saw all those kids in the dorm flapping and waving their hands around, I thought I had been dropped down in the loony bin."

"You sign so well now," I said. "If the teachers won't allow sign language, how'd you learn?"

She shrugged again and pointed to her eyes. "Watched the other kids till I picked it up," she explained. "That's what everybody does, unless they're lucky and have deaf parents who teach them at home."

A long time passed before anyone mentioned going to bed. "We better sneak back," Belinda finally signed with a sigh. "Miss Hinkle will be flashing the lights early tomorrow for us to go out and practice that awful Maypole dance."

Hattie groaned and held her nose.

Mary Alice, the shyest one of the group, broke in with a flurry of her small hands. "At least she's not making us sing this time."

I repeated her sign more slowly, waving my right hand in front of my left palm like a conductor, my eyes wide with disbelief. "*Sing*? What do you mean *sing*?"

"They always make us sing for the Parents' Day

programs," she signed. "'The Star-Spangled Banner,' Christmas carols. Songs like that. . . . One of the teachers leads us and plays the piano, but my brother—he's hearing—he says we sound terrible. Like dogs barking."

Hattie snickered. "Good," she signed.

Mary Alice looked offended. She poked out her lip in a pout. "I hate to sing. Especially that 'Star-Spangled Banner' song. Even the Maypole is better than that."

"We're not doing it," I cut in abruptly.

They all stopped.

"Doing what?" Belinda asked.

The notion had come to me out of the blue, but just signing the words filled me with determination. "We're not doing the Maypole dance."

Hattie whooped and threw up her arms in a cheer.

"We're not?" Mary Alice asked fearfully. "What do you mean? What are we doing instead?"

"Something great," I gestured, my hands tingling with newfound power. "Something different. Something *signed*."

It took a few seconds for my idea to sink in, but slowly, a glimmer of excitement began to creep across their faces. An uncertain glimmer, but a glimmer all the same.

My stomach fluttered with butterflies. Now I just needed to come up with it. Something great. Something different. Something *signed*.

22

I hardly slept that night. Hour after hour ideas flitted through my head like brightly colored birds against a dark sky—too exotic, too wild to rein in. I had twelve girls and barely more than twenty-four hours to get ready for the Jubilee. I needed an idea that was not only great and different but practical, too, or else our performance would be bound for disaster, just like the doomed dummy of Birthmark Baines.

With my sheet twisting in knots around my ankles, I drifted in and out of sleep, muddling through restless half-dreams. First there was Miss Hinkle turning into Mrs. Fernley, meticulously enunciating another word list as she stood in front of an endless field of beds. "Integrity!" she called out through ruby-painted lips. "Say it! Like this! Integrity!"

Then came Margaret and Mother and Abe. They were standing on the altar of Saint Jude's Church for the Deaf with their lips stubbornly squeezed tight, holding hands and humming "The Star-Spangled Banner."

But somehow, as I floundered awake for the third or fourth time that night, I had it. My idea. Of course I was too excited to fall asleep again after that. Through an open space under one of the tall window shades, I could see a tinge of pink light creeping into the sky. I untangled myself from the bedclothes and sneaked through the rows of sleeping girls back to the shower room, where I paced and practiced for another hour or more, until the lights in the dormitory flashed their rude wake-up call.

By the time Miss Hinkle sought me out that morning, I was bleary-eyed but dressed and ready for the day. "I'm entrusting this to you," she said, laying her precious clipboard in my hands. "They want me over at the school office right away, but you'll find everything you need written there. The weaving patterns. The girls' names listed beside their assigned ribbon color. Don't worry. I'll be sure to check on you throughout the day." With an arched eyebrow, she added, "Good luck, Miss Davis. And remember, speaking and lip reading only for those girls. *No signs.* It's for their own good."

She turned to leave, and after sticking out my

tongue at the back of her head, I hurried off to the dining hall to join the other girls for breakfast. I didn't even attempt to search for Daddy in the crowded cafeteria. There was too much to do. Belinda, Hattie, and Mary Alice had saved me a place at a table in the corner, and we huddled over the clipboard as I scribbled out the specifics of our routine on a fresh piece of paper.

Mary Alice immediately started to gnaw her lower lip. "We're going to get in trouble, aren't we?" she signed worriedly, checking over her shoulder to see whether anyone was watching.

Hattie's eyes shone with a crafty glint. "Are you kidding? Look who's teaching us." She poked my arm. "The Reverend's daughter. We're safe as long as she's in charge."

I grinned along with Hattie. She was right. Daddy was a hero at ASD. How could they punish us just for signing—an art Daddy had always taught with pride and used to reach out to deaf people all across the South?

With Mary Alice feeling somewhat reassured, Belinda darted across the dining room and brought back her sister, a studious-looking high school girl who wore silver-framed spectacles and quickly promised to keep our secret. She sat down to join our huddle and within a few minutes had helped us work out the trickier parts of our performance. By the time the kitchen manager came over to fuss at us for leaving all that oatmeal congealing in our bowls, we had already formulated a Wrinkle-proof plan of attack.

Three times that day our plan was put to the test. We took turns on lookout duty, and whenever Miss Hinkle happened to stride by the front lawn herding small groups of visitors on tours of the campus, she saw nothing more than twelve schoolgirls marching in a circle around the Maypole.

"That's right," I called out loudly, twirling my pointer finger in the air, and on cue the girls began to slide and cut around one another like spinning tops. "Weeeaaave!" I shouted. "In and out. Over and under. Weeeeave!" Thank goodness Miss Hinkle was too preoccupied to worry about why her students were circling the pole without a single ribbon clutched in their hands.

I didn't begin to have real misgivings about our performance until dinner that evening, when I looked down our table in the dining hall and saw all the girls sagging over their dinner trays. We had been practicing for hours in the drippy August heat, anxiously swooping into Maypole formation whenever a staff member ventured past and peered too closely. And still we weren't ready.

Then Belinda came back from clearing her tray with disturbing news. "She told," Belinda signed urgently as she squeezed in next to me. "My dumb sister. She told."

"Told who?" I asked, trying to keep my hands low.

Mary Alice leaned forward, almost tipping over her water glass. Hattie thumped her fist on the table. Now all the other girls were watching.

Belinda winced. "Two of her friends," she answered. "They say they want to meet with you. In the janitor's closet along the back hall."

"Meet with me?" I almost exclaimed out loud. "Why?"

"I'm not sure," Belinda signed miserably. "But they want you to be there in five minutes."

I swallowed hard. "Okay," I said, and reluctantly pushed myself up from the table.

"You're going?" Hattie signed.

Mary Alice was wringing her hands between signs. "What do they want? You think they're going to tell on us?"

The words and letters nearly shot to my fingertips. *How in the heck am I supposed to know?* But I forced myself to smile instead. "It will be all right," I signed. "I'll meet you back at the dormitory."

Then I picked up my tray and headed off to find the janitor's closet.

A few minutes later I was almost skipping as I scurried along the back corridor of Manning Hall after my rendezvous with the high schoolers. They were seniors, and they actually wanted to help us—

Belinda's sister and a clever boy who ran the broom-making shop, and another girl who had been stuck in the sewing room for three days, tailoring costumes for various numbers in the Jubilee.

All day long I had been stewing over how to re-rig the Maypole for our performance, but I had been too busy with practice to give this and other nagging details much thought. Now, like good fairies, the high school kids had spirited one of my main worries away by promising to transform the Maypole that very night after lights out. As we sat wedged among the smelly jumble of mops and buckets and cleaning supplies, the boy had even thumped me on the back and congratulated me for my idea. "G-U-T-S," he had spelled out happily on his fingers. "I like that. You got G-U-T-S."

I found a side door leading out of Manning Hall and was so elated over the sudden turn of events that I burst outside and almost ran smack-dab into my father. He had been rounding the corner of a boxwood bush, intent on some mission of his own.

"Augusta!" he cried out loud. "I was just coming to see you in the dormitory. Where have you been?"

I gave him a quick hug and then stood back to scold him. "Where have *I* been? Where have *you* been? The only time I've seen you since we got here is up on the stage." I hunched one shoulder like Quasimodo and took a few lurching steps.

Daddy laughed. "I'm sorry," he said, throwing up

his hands. "There's so much to do. And so many visitors and old students and important men in education coming for the Jubilee. They all want to talk, talk, talk." He waggled his finger in front of his mouth.

My insides churned queasily at the mention of who would be in the audience the next day watching our surprise performance.

"What about Abe?" I asked anxiously. For two days the thought of how we had left him, so lonely and forlorn at the empty Negro school, had been plaguing me like a toothache or a sharp stone in my shoe. "Have you had a chance to go back and check on him?"

Daddy shook his head. "No. I thought I might get over there today or this evening sometime. But now Mr. Snider and his parents have just arrived, and they want to meet with me over in the chapel."

"Mr. Snider?" I tried not to make a horrible face. "He's here, too?"

"Yes. Remember Mr. Snider? He and his parents have come all the way from Georgia."

I remembered him only too well, with his fawning manners and striped bow tie, bribing Daddy into traveling even more by giving him that darn Packard.

"His parents were students at ASD back in the early days," Daddy was saying. "It's wonderful they could make the trip at their age."

Daddy must have noticed I wasn't paying attention any longer. "How are you coming with the May-pole dance?" he asked. "I heard you've been put in charge. Miss Hinkle says you're doing a fine job."

I forced out a smile and bobbed my head up and down.

"Want me to walk you back to the dormitory?" he asked.

"That's okay," I signed. "You better go meet with Mr. Snider."

Daddy kissed me on my cheek. "See you tomorrow at the Jubilee," he told me.

Somehow I managed to nod again and fight back the urge to grab Daddy's arm and tell him everything.

When I got back to Graves Hall, the girls were all waiting for me, perched on the edges of their beds or lingering near the door. I was glad Miss Hinkle had secluded herself in her room, or she would have seen all the girls dashing over to find out the news.

Their hands fluttered around me. "What?" they signed. "What happened?"

My tale of the secret meeting in the janitor's closet with three seniors was enough to send a fresh current of energy zinging through our group.

"Let's practice tonight in the shower room," Hattie signed. "After lights out."

"Good idea," Belinda said, and a few of the other girls clapped their hands.

Mary Alice cut in with her usual word of warning. "We can't all go at once."

"We can practice in shifts," I suggested. I pointed to Belinda. "You go first with three girls. When Belinda's done, Hattie takes three more. Then Mary Alice with the last three. Okay? I'll stand watch."

By midnight we were ready, with only a few minor bobbles here and there. Yet as I fell, weary and triumphant, into bed, there was still one last worry drifting back and forth like a tiny ghost in my mind.

Abe.

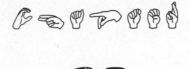

23

**Impulsiveness:
Resulting from or produced by
impulse rather than by reflection;
unpremeditated.**

Example: In an act of extreme
impulsiveness, Gussie Davis set out
for the Alabama School for the Negro
Deaf, hoping to rescue a small boy from
loneliness and despair.

M rs. Fernley would have been appalled. I could
even hear her voice scolding in my head as I
sneaked up the steps of the school bus. "Haven't you
learned anything?" the voice nagged. "Haven't your
past actions taught you anything about the dreadful
consequences of *impulsiveness?*"

But how could I resist? The bus was parked like a chariot in the main driveway, with a line of deaf folks dressed in their Sunday finest waiting to board. And as the girls and I passed by on our way across campus that morning, Miss Hinkle had stopped to talk with the bus driver. A jolt of excitement had rushed through me when I heard her mention the Negro school. "Yes, Mr. Lindermeyer has agreed to give any interested visitors a tour of the new buildings over there," she was saying. "I suppose they've been reading about the construction in the newspapers and want to see it for themselves. But bring everyone back here directly. The Jubilee begins right after lunch."

I nudged Belinda, who was walking beside me. "You all go on over to the printing press without me," I signed with my hands close to my chest. "The boys over there will show you how to fold the programs for this afternoon. I'll catch up later, okay?"

"Where are you going?" she asked.

I held my finger to my lips. "Don't worry. I'll be back in plenty of time for the show."

It was surprisingly simple to duck around the high hedge and wait until Miss Hinkle was gone, then fall into line behind the cheerful alumni. They were so eager to greet one another and catch up on old times that I was able to slip into a spot in the back row without attracting the slightest bit of attention. Whenever anyone happened to glance my way, I fixed my face in a casual expression and leaned toward the couple who sat in front of me, pretending I belonged to them.

As the bus rumbled toward the front gates, I sneaked a look out at the Maypole. I could barely keep from cackling at the sight of it. Nothing looked any different, but Belinda's sister had pulled me aside at breakfast that morning and assured me the new rigging was in place. She and her friends had kept their promise, sneaking into the sewing room after lights out to fashion a fresh set of ribbons. I couldn't imagine how they had attached and bound the new ones to the pole so cleverly in the dark. Even Miss Hinkle, unless she inspected closely, would never detect that the colors had mysteriously changed overnight.

Out on the lawn students swarmed like worker bees, setting up rows of folding chairs and welcome banners. By now the intermediate girls would be busy in the printing office, folding the programs that listed each selection of entertainment for the Jubilee.

"Don't forget, you girls will be performing first," Miss Hinkle had reminded us before we set off that morning. "You'll see your names listed right at the top of the program under 'A May Day Tribute.'"

I could tell Hattie was ready to explode with laughter. But she clamped her teeth over her bottom lip. And Mary Alice, looking woozy with fear, had closed her eyes and waited for the moment to pass. So far all of the girls in our group had managed to contain themselves. It was a miracle. Our plan was actually working.

Now there was just one thing left for me to do. I needed to persuade Mr. Vincent to let Abe come with me to the Jubilee. Then, hopefully, Abe would understand how sorry I felt, how he hadn't been abandoned after all.

"Is that you, Miss Davis?" I heard someone call from several rows up. I felt my body go rigid with alarm.

I couldn't believe it. It was *him*—that doggone pest Mr. Snider. Why was he always turning up to catch me in my most difficult situations?

I wanted to slide down in my seat like a lump of melted butter. But Mr. Snider was already lurching toward me in his seersucker suit and bright red bow tie, gripping the seat backs for balance. He dropped into the empty spot across the aisle. "What a pleasant surprise, Miss Davis!" he drawled, practically shouting over the rattle of the bus on the bumpy road. "Your father said you were helping out at the school this week. But I didn't expect to find you here. What are you up to? Off to give another humming concert?"

He belted out a hearty laugh.

I could feel the blood flaming to my cheeks, but somehow I managed to cough out a chuckle. "No, no humming this time," I said.

"Are you along for the tour?"

"Yep. I mean *yes*. That's right," I babbled. "I'm along for the tour."

Mr. Snider was studying me, clearly mystified. What an odd duck, he must have been thinking.

Still, I couldn't tell him the truth. First he had caught me humming in church, and now here I was, the Reverend's daughter, on a mission to bring a colored boy to the Jubilee. Something told me Mr. Snider might not approve of including Abe in the celebration.

But there was no chance for me to find out for sure. Before we had rounded the next corner, Mr. Snider was pointing out his wobbly, gray-haired parents and sending word from one seat to the next that Reverend Davis's daughter had joined the group for a tour of the Negro school. Soon all the passengers on the bus were turning around to beam at me and sign their hellos.

By the time we bumped down the long gravel drive and pulled to a stop, my face ached from smiling so hard. Mr. Vincent was waiting for us on the steps of the main building. Naturally, he looked surprised when he saw me file off the bus behind all those adults.

"Wait a minute," he said in a teasing voice. "I thought I gave you a tour already."

"I wanted to see more," I said.

Mr. Snider was watching too closely for me to ask my real question: *Where's Abe?* I had no choice but to follow along with the group through the silent hallways to one freshly scrubbed classroom after another, each smelling of floor wax and Murphy's oil soap. In every room, as the visitors nodded and murmured their approval, I could hear the wall clocks ticking away the minutes until the Jubilee. Ten thirty-five . . . ten forty-three . . . ten fifty-two. But there was no sign of Abe anywhere—not along the hallways or stairways, not on the dirt playing field beyond the classroom windows, not even among the maze of bunk beds in the boys' dormitory. At last I spotted a single clue—the corner of his canvas duffel peeking from under a neatly made bottom bunk in the corner.

Abe had to be around somewhere, and I had to find him fast. Mr. Vincent was leading the group out front again while doing his best to humor Mr. Snider, who kept stopping to interrupt with his grand pronouncements. "The state of Alabama has bestowed a marvelous gift!" he bellowed to no one in particular. "What a marvelous gift this school is for the colored folk of Alabama!"

As everyone finally moved toward the foyer, I lagged behind and ducked between two rows of bunk beds, hiding until Mr. Snider's voice had faded. Then I took a deep breath and sprinted back through the dormitory toward a rear exit door we had passed earlier.

I needed to find the school cafeteria again. Mr. Vincent hadn't bothered to show us the kitchen on our tour, but I was sure I had heard running water and the clank of pots when we passed through the small dining hall. And I remembered Mr. Vincent saying that a school cook would be watching over Abe until the other students arrived.

Darting along the back of the buildings like a fugitive from one of my Nancy Drew books, I made my way to the place where I thought the kitchen might be. "Wouldn't you know?" I whispered in exasperation as I leaned against the building for a few seconds to catch my breath. The windows were several inches too high to get a good view inside. I stretched up on my tiptoes, gripping the stone ledge with my fingers. Still I couldn't see a thing through the heavy screen. So I bent my knees and jumped, and jumped again, trying to get a better look.

I heard Abe before I saw him. That familiar hee-haw of laughter. It was coming from behind me somewhere. I whipped around and there he stood, giggling over the jack-in-the-box performance I had just put on, grinning wide enough to show his gums and every tooth left in his mouth.

"Abe!" I squealed. I must have run right past him earlier. He had been playing among the droopy branches of a nearby hydrangea bush. The knees of his trousers were dusty, and he held a wooden toy train in each hand.

I could have hugged him, but I didn't want to scare him away. Instead, I rested my hands on the tops of his bony shoulders and squeezed.

"Abe," I said again, and smiled. Suddenly, I remembered to make the name sign my father had invented—the outline of Lincoln's stovepipe hat in the air.

Abe smiled back. Then he held out the toy trains for me to see. I took the larger one, a steam engine, and turned it over in my palm. It was handmade, with a smokestack, notches for windows, and tiny wheels that really turned. And two initials were etched on the wooden surface underneath—a V and an L. Vincent Lindermeyer. He must have made the trains for Abe to help take his mind off home.

"Toot, toot," I said and rolled the toy engine back and forth over my palm.

No sooner had the sound left my lips than I heard a real horn beeping off in the distance.

I gasped. "Abe, that's the school bus! They must be looking for me."

He blinked. Of course he didn't understand, but I could see a spark of fear flare up in his eyes as he watched the worry spreading across my face.

"Come," I gestured, and put my arm around his shoulder to guide him along. The horn beeped again, three honks this time, longer and more urgent. "We've got to go. You need to come with me."

Abe tugged away, and my heart sank until I realized that he was rushing back only to fetch the toy trains he had left under the hydrangea bush. He stuffed them in his pockets, then hitched up his saggy pants and trotted to my side, ready to go.

As I grabbed Abe's hand, I came close to hugging him again, or maybe even bursting into tears. I didn't deserve it—for this little boy to trust me enough to follow me anywhere, even though I had been so mean to him.

When Abe and I came trotting around the side of the school, they were all sitting on the bus waiting for me—everyone but Mr. Snider, who stood out in the driveway with his fists on his hips. He had taken off his seersucker coat, and there were dark wet patches staining the underarms of his shirt.

"Where on earth have you been, young lady?" he cried, his gaze raking back and forth from Abe to me. "And who's this little ragamuffin? Mr. Lindermeyer just went over to the dormitory for the second time to search for you."

Through the bus window, I could see Mr. Snider's ancient parents peering at me in distress, as if I had suddenly sprouted devil's horns and a barbed tail.

"I'm sorry," I panted. "This is my friend Abe. I

had to go find him. He's coming to the Jubilee with us."

Mr. Snider stared at me, flabbergasted. His parents must have read my lips through the window, because in the next instant, there were more concerned faces pressing up against the glass, and signs flying to and fro like Ping-Pong balls.

I was glad to see Mr. Vincent come hurrying back from the dormitory. When he spotted me, he raised his face to the sky in silent thanks. "There you are!" he exclaimed out loud. "I was starting to worry."

"You *should* be worried," Mr. Snider said, planting his fists on his hips again. "Miss Davis has the strange notion that she's bringing this fellow along to the Jubilee. I know her father would never approve of such an idea." He glanced at his watch impatiently. "And it's getting late. We should be back at ASD by now."

Mr. Vincent's eyes widened as he took in Mr. Snider's words. He turned to me.

"Why can't Abe go?" I asked in a rush before he could say anything. Abe stared up at me in wonder as I signed, my hands jerky with emotion. "He won't be any trouble. And Daddy won't mind giving him a ride back. Abe's been here for three whole days, with not much to do and no kids to keep him company. And there'll be all sorts of great things for him to see at the Jubilee—tumbling and dancing and costumes, and the senior boys are going to juggle, and we're going t—"

Mr. Snider cut in. "This is a celebration to honor Miss Benton," he said firmly. "The principal of the *white* school."

I opened my mouth to argue, but Mr. Vincent laid a quieting hand on my shoulder. He turned to Mr. Snider. "You all go on ahead," he said in a calm voice. "I don't want you to be late, and Gussie and I can work this out between the two of us in my office. I'll give her a ride over in the school car when we're done."

"But—"

Mr. Vincent held up his hand, and a surge of panic welled in my throat. I didn't have time to sit in his office and discuss things. I needed to rush back and get the girls ready for our performance. But the driver had already started the engine, and Mr. Snider was mounting the steps of the bus, still shaking his head in blustery disapproval.

24

I thought I might scream. As the clock on the wall over his head clicked off the precious minutes, Mr. Vincent sat with his chin in his hand, just thinking. Abe was making soft growling sounds in his throat as he chugged his steam engine down one leg of Mr. Vincent's desk, around my feet, and up the other leg. Then Abe squeezed past my knees, pushing his train through the forest of handmade wooden objects spread across the desktop. A pen stand decorated with fancy whittled designs. Sleek bins carved with the words IN and OUT. Even wooden bookends crafted into the shape of acorns, maybe to honor the oak tree that had supplied the wood.

I flapped my hand to get his attention. "He's just one little boy," I said.

"I know," Mr. Vincent signed, tapping his fingers to his forehead.

"No one will even notice." I could hear my voice turning desperate.

Mr. Vincent sighed and gave me a pitying look. "Believe me, Gussie. They'll notice."

"I'll take full responsibility!"

He rose from his chair with another sigh and turned to gaze out the window, still thinking.

I let my open palms flop to my lap in frustration.

Abe was bumping and zooming his train into another one of the obstacles on Mr. Vincent's desk. He picked it up and with a little grunt of amusement, laid it in my cupped palms. It was a box, and something about the dark, satiny wood was familiar. I turned the box over. Mr. Vincent had made it. His telltale initials—VL—were carved into the bottom.

I bent closer to examine it. The lid of the box was shaped like a heart, with a perfect replica of a hand carved across it. But there were deep grooves chiseled into the fingers and the wrist of the hand. A piece of the lid was missing. Abe watched as I quietly lifted the lid. Inside was a lock of white-blond hair.

With a sharp hitch of breath, I closed the box and raised it from my lap just as Mr. Vincent was turning around.

The words flew out of me before I could stop them. "Miss Grace has the other hand! I thought hers was just a paperweight, but it's the other half of the sign!"

"What?" Mr. Vincent said, staring at my mouth.

I set the box on his desk and crossed my hands over my heart—the sign for love. "She has it on her desk. Just like you."

With a squawk of laughter, Abe imitated me, pressing his small grubby palms over his heart.

"She has it?" Mr. Vincent signed. "The other hand?" A wild look of hope lit up his face.

I nodded. He didn't ask more questions after that but took the box in his hands, lifted the lid, and gaped at the lock of Miss Grace's hair as if he was seeing it for the first time.

I frantically checked the clock again. Only forty minutes left till the show.

I stood up. No one was going to stop me. ASD was only a couple of miles down the road. Abe and I could walk there, or run, and still be at the school in time. I could feel my knees quiver as I caught hold of Abe's hand.

"Mr. Vincent," I said. "We have to leave. They're depending on me."

Thank heaven for Miss Grace and the power of love. At last Mr. Vincent said, "All right," and grabbed his keys to take us, both me and Abe, to the Jubilee.

Like lots of people, I suppose, I had always felt a little numb singing the national anthem. At school assemblies and ball games and choir concerts, the words would pour out of my mouth in a senseless mush.

Osaycanyouseebythedawn'searlylightwhatsoproudlywe-hail'd . . .

But *signing* "The Star-Spangled Banner" was different, especially in front of hundreds of people expecting to see nothing but a Maypole dance. We had started our performance routinely enough, each taking a ribbon and circling around and around until the red, white, and blue streamers blossomed and were spinning like a giant pinwheel.

But then we all let go and the ribbons floated down, hiding the pole under a curtain of color. Still in our circle, we kept our arms raised and turned to face the audience. For a few long seconds, everyone stared at our poised, empty hands, until finally we began to sing.

This was something very new for ASD—a ring of students singing together with their hands. It was new for me, too. For the first time, as the words of the song welled up through my fingers and came to life in the air, I felt as if I was truly a part of Mother and Daddy's miraculous world.

Once we had made it through "twilight's last gleaming," I peeked over at Mary Alice. To my astonishment, she didn't appear the least bit timid or afraid. In fact, she had lifted her chin proudly, almost defiantly, as if each sign she made was sweet revenge on her little brother, somewhere out there in the audience, who had once compared the girls' singing voices to the sound of barking dogs.

Seeing that tilt of Mary Alice's chin gave me the nerve to look out at the spectators while I signed. Just as I expected, Miss Hinkle sat seething in her folding chair in the middle of the front row, each muscle taut as a tightrope. Over the grassy lawn, her eyes blazed a path straight to me, and for an instant, the memory of her strict instructions—"And remember. No signing for those girls. It's for their own good!"—crowded out all the other thoughts in my head.

I scanned the audience for Daddy, my hands wavering a bit. Where was he? What had happened to Abe? When Mr. Vincent and I had finally found my father among the crowds of people milling about on the lawn, there were only a few minutes left to spare before the show. And of course Mr. Snider was already there at Daddy's side, tattling away about my "disruptive and outlandish actions" during the tour of the Negro school.

"You see?" Mr. Snider had said to Daddy as soon as I had come hurrying up with Abe gripping my arm. "It's just as I told you. Your daughter actually thinks we are going to allow this boy to stay for Miss Benton's celebration."

There hadn't been time for me to stay and argue more. All I could do was push Abe toward Daddy and hope for the best as I ran to get ready for our performance.

Now I sneaked a desperate glance at Belinda, struggling not to fall behind the rest of the group. We were at her favorite part—"the rocket's red glare, the bombs bursting in air."

"Can we do that again?" she had kept begging during our practice sessions. Now I could see her flushed face glowing almost as bright as her hair as she raised her graceful arms and used her fingers to mimic a shower of fireworks raining down.

A movement in one of the back rows caught my eye just as my hands found their way into the song again.

. . . *gave proof through the night that our flag was still there.*

It was my father. He was standing up. And there was Abe, standing on the folding chair right beside him. Daddy must have lifted him up so that he could get a better view. Over the rows of heads, I could see Abe laughing as he copied Daddy's every move, placing his hand over his heart for the second time that day.

I found myself smiling from ear to ear, too, as our circle of girls burst into the final phrases of the anthem.

O say does that star-spangled banner yet wave
O'er the land of the free . . .

Then another man in the back row got to his feet, and a ripple of movement traveled through the audience as more and more folks decided to rise from their seats.

"Thank you, Daddy!" I wanted to shout with my hands. *Thank you, thank you.* Thank you for being so different. Thank you for spending all those hours on the train and in that hand-me-down Packard, trying to spread your message. Thank you for letting stray souls like Abe and Mary Alice and Belinda and Hattie and me know that we really do have an important place in this great big land of the free and home of the brave.

No one clapped right away when we finished the song. Maybe they weren't sure whether we were done or not. But in the front row, there was an elderly lady with soft white hair pulled back in a bun who stood and took a step forward just as we lowered our hands to our sides. I was surprised when she fixed her watery blue gaze on me.

"That was very beautiful," she called out in a quavering but firm voice. "If you wouldn't mind, I think we would all like to see that again."

I nodded, gradually realizing that I was meeting the famous Miss Emmeline Benton at last. She remained standing for our second round of the national anthem, and oh, my, I couldn't help it. I couldn't help breaking into a gloating grin when I spotted Miss Hinkle and then Mr. Snider slowly but surely rising to their feet.

25

On the way home the next day, my father stopped at that same dusty service station to fill the Packard's tank and "rest his eyes" for a bit. In the shade of the cottonwoods, I tapped Daddy's arm just as he was sinking back against the seat.

He opened one eye and turned his head to face me.

"Do you think Mr. Vincent will really come to Birmingham soon to visit us like he promised?" I asked.

"Sure," Daddy said. "He'll come."

"Maybe this week sometime?" I asked.

Daddy shook his head sleepily. "Not this week. His students begin arriving tomorrow, remember?"

"Oh, that's right." I nodded.

I tapped Daddy's arm again. "What about next weekend?"

He gripped the steering wheel and finally rousted

himself from his comfortable spot, smiling wanly at my stubborn questions. "Maybe so. But I won't even be in Birmingham next weekend. I'll be preaching in Jasper. Although," he added slowly, with a hint of mystery in his voice, "I don't think I'm the one Mr. Vincent really wants to visit."

I cocked my head to one side. "What do you mean?"

"I think he'd like to see Grace Homewood."

Just like that, Daddy said it, as if he was commenting on the weather.

I couldn't stop my eyebrows from shooting upward. "Really?" I asked, as if I had never heard of such a notion. "How do you know?"

"I knew them both as students, and later, when they started working at ASD. They were sweethearts once."

I leaned forward, my voice hushed. "What happened?"

Daddy shook his head. "It was sad. Grace's parents didn't want them to be together. They were afraid that if their daughter married a deaf man, their grandchildren would be deaf, too." He shook his head again. "For some hearing people, that's too frightening a prospect."

"You knew all along?" I cried. "That they loved each other? Couldn't you have done something? Something to change her parents'—"

Daddy held up his fist, twisting it back and forth

in a firm sign for "no." "It's not always my place to step in. Besides," he added, crossing his hands over his heart, "true love has a way of working out on its own, with or without a minister's help."

With that pronouncement, my father tipped his head back against the seat and quickly drifted off to sleep. I gazed over the dashboard toward the bean field. This time I wasn't the least bit impatient during Daddy's catnap. My mind was too busy spinning far-fetched possibilities round and round.

Back at home that evening, the possibilities didn't seem quite so far-fetched—especially after Miss Grace nodded hello and honored me with a tiny smile of forgiveness when we happened to pass on the stairs. After dinner, while Mother and Daddy lingered at the table signing, I wandered up to my father's office and sat at the window in his swivel chair. Across the hall, Mrs. Fernley was playing an opera piece I had never heard before. As I listened to the soprano's voice floating through the third floor, I looked down and imagined the magical scenes of my own little opera playing out on our shadowy driveway below.

I could see it so clearly: a taxicab pulling into the streetlamp's circle of light and Mr. Vincent striding up the walk with the heart-shaped box tucked in his pocket, ready to retrieve that missing piece.

And I could see my sisters as they arrived home from Texas. I would run out to the driveway to greet them. I would hug Nell, and Margaret, too, and resist the temptation to blurt out my latest news: that I had actually directed a signing performance at the Jubilee, and as a reward, Mother had invited me to come back to Saint Jude's and join the deaf choir on Sunday mornings.

And I could see the Packard pulling out of our driveway again and again during the busy falls and winters and springs to come. But from now on, at least once a month, I would be at Daddy's side on the front seat, on my way to Talladega to visit Abe and my other new friends at the Alabama School for the Deaf.

And far beyond the glow of the streetlamp, I could see Vulcan's torch shining over Red Mountain— what else but a brilliant and hopeful shade of green?

All right, I thought. *I'm ready.* I spun around in Daddy's swivel chair, wheeled back to his desk, and rolled a clean sheet of paper into the Smith Corona. This time I didn't need the Funk and Wag or any other dictionary to finish my word-list assignment for Mrs. Fernley. I was ready to define "integrity" all on my own.

Author's Note

My mother once told me a story that helped me understand some of the complexities of growing up as a hearing child of deaf parents. She was sitting in class in sixth or seventh grade when she happened to drop her pencil on the floor. Joe Milazzo, who was the object of all the girls' secret crushes and would one day be voted best-looking boy in the senior class, reached down and returned her pencil. Without thinking, my mother made the sign for the words "Thank you," touching the fingertips of her right hand lightly to her lips.

Joe turned a bright shade of red and grinned at her in utter surprise. Up and down the rows of desks, her classmates were grinning, too. Everyone thought that shy Roberta Fletcher had just blown a kiss to none other than Joseph Milazzo. My mother thought she might die of mortification.

Over the years I asked my mother many questions about the Fletcher family. She poured forth one tale after another about life in this colorful southern household with a deaf father who worked as a traveling minister, a deaf mother who took on the burdens of his far-flung congregations, four lively hearing children, and a parade of eccentric ladies who rented the extra bedrooms to help the family make ends meet. From these stories, this novel was born.

While many scenes in this book are borrowed straight from my mother's recollections, others have been conjured from my imagination. Instead of the four siblings of the Fletcher family, I decided to grace the Davis family with three daughters—mainly because I have three daughters of my own and have become well-acquainted with the joys and sorrows of the sisterhood triangle.

Perhaps the character in the book who is shown in the truest light is Reverend Davis, whose portrayal is based on my grandfather, Robert Capers Fletcher. Whenever I think of summer visits from Pop, I picture him sitting next to me at our kitchen table, teaching me how to sign the alphabet. He never seemed to tire of guiding me through those twenty-six simple signs. He lingered fondly over each letter, demonstrating first and then smiling as he shared clever hints to help me recall the proper hand positions. "Pretend you're picking up a feather," he instructed when we came to the letter *F*. "That's it—*F* for feather." For G, it was always, "Hold your hand like this, like you're shooting a gun. Remember G for gun."

After several practice sessions with Pop, I could

fly through the alphabet without any reminders. "Phew!" he would exclaim and shake his head as if he had never encountered such speed and dexterity.

Once he was satisfied with my fingerspelling, Pop began to teach me signs for words, always adding an entertaining explanation of what the origins of the gesture might be. For example, to make the sign for "girl," he explained, you brush your thumb along the side of your cheek, representing the bonnet strings that girls in the olden days used to tie under their chin.

Years later, when I introduced my grandfather to the man I would marry, barely ten minutes had passed before Pop seated my future husband at that same kitchen table to slowly and patiently teach him the sign for *A*, then *B*, then *C*. . . .

I laughed at the familiar sight, but I wasn't surprised. I had always known my grandfather was a natural-born teacher. What I didn't know, until I began the research for this book, was how vast the scope of his teachings had been.

Like the character of Reverend Davis, my grandfather worked as an Episcopal missionary to the deaf, traveling by train to organize and preach to congregations spread across nine states. For twenty-five years, with the help of his faithful wife, Estelle, he kept up a relentless pace of travel, returning to Birmingham for just one week a month to tend to the needs of his family and his home church, Saint John's Church for

The Fletcher family's real-life experiences inspired many of the events in this novel. Pictured above are the Reverend Robert Fletcher and his wife, Estelle, and their four children—Louise and John (at back), with their younger sisters, Georgianna (left) and Roberta (right) in matching outfits.

the Deaf (fictionalized and renamed Saint Jude's in this book). The constant travel took its toll. Chronic stomach ulcers and a severe bout of pneumonia finally forced my grandfather to confine his mission work to the state of Alabama.

From the 1930s to the early 1970s—a time when society ignored and often shunned "the handicapped"—Reverend Fletcher's services provided a bright ray of light in the lives of hundreds of deaf church members, both white and black. They eagerly awaited his arrival each month, traveling from the nearest cities or isolated country towns to see him deliver his wise sermons, perform baptisms, and conduct marriages and funeral ceremonies—all in graceful sign language.

While many schools for deaf children were teaching generations of pupils that it was shameful to sign and that they should disguise their disability by learning to speak like hearing people, Reverend Fletcher taught his students to be proud of their unique language. He mesmerized his audiences with his vivid signed storytelling. But most of all, his mission centered on bringing deaf people out of the shadows and helping them move freely between the worlds of the hearing and the deaf. At heart, my grandfather was a matchmaker, delighting in pairing those he met during his travels with the perfect mate, a steady job, or an affordable home.

Pop passed away in 1988. What I wouldn't give for the chance to sit with him once more at that old kitchen table and show him how smoothly I can sign the alphabet. But thankfully, though both my grandparents are gone, there are still hands singing everywhere to remind us of the rich gifts that they and their fellow pioneers in the deaf community left behind.

Thanks

I would like to thank Douglas Baynton for his generosity in providing insight about deaf culture and for his sensitive and expert critique of the original manuscript for this book. Thanks are also owed to Lynn Edge and Garland Reeves for their tours of landmarks and their gracious answers to my flurry of questions related to Birmingham history, and to the Reverend Jay Croft and the members of Saint John's Church for the Deaf for welcoming me into their lovely sanctuary. Peggy Rupp, Don Veasey at the Birmingham Public Library, and Jean Bergey at Gallaudet University helped to fill in the blanks about important historical details. I am also indebted to Karyn Zweifel and the staff at the Alabama Institute for Deaf and Blind for providing valuable information about the history of the school, as well as Maude Nelson, Olen "the Professor" Tate, and his wife, Agnes, for sharing firsthand accounts of their experiences as students and staff members at the Alabama School for the Deaf.

I am grateful to Virginia Buckley for her editorial

wisdom and her faith in this project from the start. And finally, I reserve my profoundest thanks for my mother and "ghost editor," Bobby Fletcher Ray, who dedicated countless hours of phone time, hunting through family archives, and reviving memories to help shape the heart of this book.